SIX CURTAINS FOR STROGANOVA

IPL Library of Crime Classics®
proudly presents
STROGANOFF IN THE BALLET
by
Caryl Brahms & S.J. Simon

A BULLET IN THE BALLET
MURDER A LA STROGANOFF
(British title: CASINO FOR SALE)
SIX CURTAINS FOR STROGANOVA

SIX CURTAINS FOR STROGANOVA

Caryl Brahms & S.J. Simon

INTERNATIONAL POLYGONICS, LTD.
New York

SIX CURTAINS FOR STROGANOVA

Originally published by J.B. Lippincott Company, as *Six Curtains for Natasha*. This edition restores the original British title.
Copyright© 1946 by Doris Abrahams and Simon Jasha Skidelsky.
Cover: Copyright© 1986 by International Polygonics, Ltd.
Library of Congress Card Catalog No. 86-81920
ISBN 0-930330-49-8

Printed and manufactured in the United States of America by Guinn Printing.
First IPL printing September 1986.
10 9 8 7 6 5 4 3 2 1

DEDICATION

TO

NINA TARAKANOVA   *Ballerina*

and

JUDY CAMPBELL   *Nightingale*

DEAR NINA AND JUDY,

You asked for a Stroganoff ballet book and since we may not write about this gallant troupe again we ask you to share the dedication.

CARYL and SKID

Not the Albany.

Note to

PROFESSORS BEAUMONT AND HASKELL

Should any ballerina in this book dance at the Maryinsky before she arrived there or after she left, the authors beg to submit that it is not their accuracy which can be held in question but Vladimir Stroganoff's memory, for which they are in no way responsible.

CHAPTER I

The first curtain was all that a curtain should be.

For one thing it came down slowly and gave the company plenty of time to line up, bow radiantly to the audience, and politely to one another. The house rose at them. It cooed, it shouted, it clapped, it waved its programmes.

After all, London had seen worse Coppélias than this—one or two.

The second curtain belonged to Swanhilda. The little Stroganova took it alone, banked in by bouquets, with more arriving. Roses and carnations from Mamoushka, orchids from Stroganoff—which was as it should be—gladioli from the corps-de-ballet (deducted from the salary), rhododendrons from Arenskaya—where had she seen that basket before? Forget-me-nots from the conductor—as though she could! She frowned. She remembered herself. She smiled radiantly and the house roared its approval.

But by the third curtain the going was heavier.

"Assez de chi-chi," said Marie Rambert, and sat firmly down.

The clapping waned. They brought on Frans and Coppelius. They brought on the conductor. He brought on the distinguished oboist. The clapping spurted, but it was only a spurt. They brought on Vladimir Stroganoff. He brought on his banker. It helped a little but not much. Then they panicked, and brought on everything they could think of including a laurel wreath belonging to the imperturbable Ernest Smithsky, who threw a temperament that was nobody's business in the wings. They went on bowing.

In the circle S. J. Simon turned on Caryl Brahms. "You brought me here," he hissed.

By the fourth curtain Arnold Haskell had stopped saying "Brava."

The fifth curtain was definitely grim. Little Stroganova still smiled radiantly and bowed herself dizzy but the Duchess was adjusting her furs, Oliver Messel had already reached the pass door and Cecil Beaton was definitely feeling for his hat. Ninette de Valois patted a relaxed Margot Fonteyn on the shoulder and Professor Beaumont, who, it was rumoured, was planning to do for Coppélia what he had already done for Giselle, closed his note-book with a snap.

And still they did not play "God save the King."

★ ★ ★

In the wings chaos had encroached on the congratulations.

"Non! Non! Non!" screamed Arenskaya, the temperamental maîtresse-de-ballet whose slightest shrill was law,

"The curtain it stay where it is. **Down!**" She pointed.

"Levez! Levez!" screamed a little old woman in black, flapping her arms in the air as though willing it to levitate. But as this failed she turned on a stage hand. "Oop! Oop!" she commanded in her fluent English. "All my life I wait for this moment," she appealed to his dazed better nature. Clearly she was a mother.

"Down," commanded Arenskaya.

"Oop," shrieked the mother.

Alone in the centre of the great stage of the Collodeum Theatre the little Stroganova looked appealingly at them over a bank of miscellaneous objects.

"Viens! Viens!" Arenskaya was beckoning.

"Stay where you am," the little black woman commanded. "Oop," she jerked the stage hand.

The stage hand disengaged himself. Who did they take him for? Solomon? He made off.

"Ah, bon," said the little woman in black. She pounced on the wheel. Arenskaya dragged her from it. They clawed.

A third pair of hands inserted themselves into the struggle and pulled the contestants apart. They were white hands, they were dimpled, and they had a different sort of ring on every finger.

"My darlings," said Vladimir Stroganoff. "Calm yourself immediate—both." He beamed at them. "Is this the moment to dispute yourselves? To-night of all nights, when we are in my dear London again, after the war so black, and make the opening triumphant and nearly enough moneys not to pay everyone. Non, non, non," he insisted. "To-morrow you tear the hair in comfort, but to-night," he patted their shoulders, "we are all the friends insep-arable. So you tell Papa Stroganoff what is the matter and rest assured that he will find a way to satisfy you both." And he beamed confidently at the stage hand who had drifted back to watch.

"She demand that the curtain go up," screamed Aren-skaya accusingly.

"She demand that the curtain stay doon," accused the small black woman. "You hear, Vladimir! Only five cur-tains and she demand that it stay doon."

"It is the common sense," screamed Arenskaya.

"It is the treachery," screamed the small black woman.

Out on the stage the little Stroganova was doing fouettés to keep herself warm.

Stroganoff pondered. "My darlings," he began, "soyez raisonable."

"Raisonable!" The small black woman quivered all over. "Moi!"

"A curtain," said Stroganoff, "is not a thing that just go up and down. It has," he pointed out, "to be demanded."

"And I demand that it stay down," said Arenskaya.

"And I," said the little black woman fiercely, "demand that you keep the promise you made to me many years ago in St. Petersburg in the name of our poor dead Tzar."

"Oh, that old promise," said Arenskaya. "He spit him of his promise."

It was a mistake. Stroganoff drew himself up.

"My word," he said, "is to me my bonds. Much better than my bonds," he remembered. "Ankara Tramways," he explained sadly.

"Is this the moment to change the subject?" demanded the small black woman. "And anyway, did I not plead with you to buy the British War Loan?"

"Soyez raisonable," said Stroganoff. "What use to me is the three per cent.?"

"And what use to me is the broken promise?" demanded the small black woman. "All my life it bring me bad luck. In Yokohama," she said accusingly, "there was the earthquake!"

"And is it my fault?" asked Stroganoff.

"Who else?" said the small black woman. "In Buenos Aires," she went on, "Anton Palook he drop the ballerina in Giselle."

"That was his custom," said Arenskaya.

"Entendu," agreed the small black woman. "But this time," she quivered all over, "it is me! You are laughing, Vladimir?"

"No, no," said Stroganoff quickly. "I am all the sympathy. Continue, my darling." He waved her on.

The small black woman rummaged among her memories. She rejected a defaulting backer, the pearls that were found again—in her dressing-case—and what Massine had said to her at Massachusetts. "In Wurtemburg," she produced, "I am dancing Lac des Cygnes and the curtain it come down and will not rise again, no—never, though we pull and we pull, and I," her voice rose to a scream, "have done but seventeen fouettés." She rounded on Stroganoff. "You promise me six curtains," she said doggedly, "and until you keep your word there is nothing but the misfortunes for us both."

Stroganoff was visibly impressed. "C'est vrai," he muttered, "did not my company arrive at Yalta au moment précis that Winston Churchill, the President, and One Other they go there too and my publicity," he shook his head sadly, "it go—poof!"

"It was the coincidence," said Arenskaya.

"It was the will of God," said the small black woman. She looked up at the curtain. "Oop," she said.

Stroganoff hesitated.

"Do you wish that history repeat itself," hissed the small black woman. "Was it not because of this that I walk out on you in Petersburg?"

"Only," pointed out Arenskaya, "you have walk back again."

But the small black woman took no notice. She had turned on Stroganoff and was confronting him like an infuriated cottage loaf.

"Nu," she said, "does the curtain go oop, or do I?"

The curtain did.

Out on the stage the little Stroganova, caught unawares, bent herself double as graciously as her hurry would permit. The applause seemed a little thin as she came up to be greeted by wave after wave of an empty crimson sea. The little argument that mamoushka had waged had taken the best part of a quarter of an hour and the only hands left to applaud belonged to Lord Streatham, press agent to the Company. There was another man with him, but he was only raising a pair of sandy eyebrows.

"Down," said Arenskaya.

This time there was no argument.

CHAPTER II

S TROGANOFF's office was the busiest place in the Collodeum Theatre. Accordingly it was situated at the end of a corridor and four flights of stairs, and the lifts had been out of order for years. Once there, however, the climber was amply rewarded. Photographs of Stroganoff festooned the wall space. Here and there a ballerina, poised on the pointes and scrawled all over with affectionate signatures, had somehow inserted herself, but in the main it was Stroganoff on the stage with his company around him, Stroganoff at the station, Stroganoff on the captain's bridge with an infuriated-looking Captain, Stroganoff in the sunshine, Stroganoff in the snows, Stroganoff with the Aga Khan, and almost, but never quite, Stroganoff on a hearthrug smiling winningly at his rattle.

But the wall above the desk was reserved for Pavlova. Stroganoff sat below her, for he liked to feel that she was watching and smiling approvingly at the arrangements he made for his Company, but there were times when he wondered.

On the desk stood a model of the Gare du Nord, delicately worked in silver and gold. It commemorated the ballet that bore its name and it had been presented to Stroganoff by its grateful choreographer, Nicholas Nevajno, on the opening night. How they had cheered! The bill did not reach Stroganoff till the following week. How his banker had cursed!

Now it was labelled "Carry with Care. This side Oop."

This morning Stroganoff was seated at his desk looking over the notices of last night's Coppélia. He read one and frowned. He read another and scowled. He read a third and tore it across.

"Mr. Stroganoff always reads all the notices himself," explained Lord Streatham sunnily.

"In America," said Stroganoff, "I read them too. They are mooch better. There we have the press ecstatic," he explained to the pair of sandy eyebrows, who had been waiting "un petit moment" quite a long time now.

Lord Streatham, who had been waiting quite a long time with him, smiled uneasily.

"On the whole," he said.

"The News Chronicle—poof!" said Stroganoff. "The Daily Telegraph—pfui! The Times, ca ne compte pas." He threw the lot of them in the waste-paper basket. "Cigar," he offered.

Fortunately the box on the table still contained one. Unfortunately Stroganoff, forgetting his purpose, lit it himself.

"Eh bien?" he turned expansively to the sandy eyebrows. "What can I do for you, my friend? The interview with the little Stroganova?"

"Well . . ." said the sandy eyebrows.

"Bon, it is arrange," said Stroganoff. "You take her to the

Savoy. I book the table now." He reached for the telephone. "And if they give me again the one in the corner where I cannot be seen," he thumped his fist, "I kick up the row that is the affair of nobody."

"Don't do that," said Lord Streatham uneasily. "Give the headwaiter a fiver."

Stroganoff pondered this. "It will be better," he decided, "if I give him tenner."

"By all means," said Lord Streatham cordially.

Stroganoff thought of something else. "You lend me?" he demanded confidently.

A shock of black hair slouched elegantly into the room, peered not very hopefully into the empty box of cigars, shook a disappointed head at the sandy eyebrows, frowned at Stroganoff, sighted Lord Streatham reluctantly extracting his wallet and brightened at once.

"Ah," said Nicholas Nevajno, choreographer of the future, "you lend me twenty pounds till next week?"

Lord Streatham looked definitely depressed.

"Or maybe," said Nevajno helpfully, "till the week after."

"Allons, allons," said Stroganoff. "We have not the time now to discuss the finance personal. If anyone borrow money in this office it is me." He stowed away the tenner. "And now you do me the favour and go," he announced, "for soon there comes one from whom I will borrow mooch money. Very mooch." He rubbed his hands.

The man with the sandy eyebrows raised both.

"It is the finance intricate," explained Stroganoff. "My ballet needs money and the man who comes he has too mooch. It is fair that he lose a little."

Lord Streatham winced.

"Lose?" said the man with the sandy eyebrows.

"It is not essential, this," said Stroganoff, "but it is very probable. But we will not weep for the rich one, mon cher, for he will have a wonderful time with my ballerinas while he is losing it and, au fond, it can only be what he expects."

"I see," said the man with the sandy eyebrows.

"Mr. Stroganoff will have his little joke," said Lord Streatham with hollow bonhomie.

"Assez," said Stroganoff. "Back to business. So you interview the little Stroganova at supper, and you remember to congratulate her on her six curtains."

"Ha!" said Nicholas Nevajno darkly. "That is what I come to see you about, Vladimir. If for Coppélia—this old-fashioned children's," his lip curled, "throwaway you have six curtains then for my concept colossal—the new one," he explained to the sandy eyebrows, "I demand twelve."

"Impossible," said Stroganoff promptly. "The stalls will be empty."

"It is not the stalls," said Nevajno, "it is the principle."

But at the word "principle," Stroganoff sighed heavily and shook a firm head.

"My friend," he said, "when two Russians discuss a principle it takes all night, and also, which is more important, all day." He looked at his watch. "The rich one is late and it is not good that he should hear too much about principle. So you please me and go. Shoo!" he said to clinch matters.

Lord Streatham went quickly.

"He has not lent me the twenty," said Nevajno. He went after him.

But the man with the sandy eyebrows settled himself more comfortably.

"Now, Mr. Stroganoff," he said.

But Stroganoff was crawling on all fours on the floor. He had unearthed a large poster and was trying to spread it flat.

"This end," he said with considerable exertion, "I fasten under the fender, so. You, mon cher, shall sit on the other so that it does not all the time get up and hit me. Here is a cushion." He flung it.

They arranged themselves, the sandy eyebrows on the poster, and Stroganoff standing back to admire.

"It is effective—no?" he asked.

The sandy eyebrows got up to look.

"But non, non," said Stroganoff. "Do not impatient yourself. Presently it will be your turn to admire, and I," he promised, "will sit on the cushion."

"Mr. Stroganoff," said the sandy eyebrows firmly while the poster rolled up over the fender, "I am not here to . . ."

The door opened. Two figures burst in, one a screaming ramrod, the other an offended steam-roller.

"Voilà!" screamed Arenskaya. "Now we shall see what Stroganoff has to say."

"Together," said the steam-roller in the suffocated voice of a mother determined to do battle to the last.

Stroganoff looked steadily out of the window. "I am busy," he said. "Go away."

"*You* are busy," said Arenskaya scornfully. "*You* are busy. I suppose it is you who teach the classes, and see to the dresses, and take the rehearsals, and make love to the electrician . . . the handsome one." She stopped reflectively.

The steam-roller seized her chance.

"If," she said, "that skinny little piece of twopence nothing can take six curtains, then it is an outrage that my daughter, who it is well known can dance her head off, is not permitted to take even one."

"From the corps-de-ballet?" asked Arenskaya sweetly.

"The corps-de-ballet," said the steam-roller from the depths of her being.

"Mais si," said Arenskaya. "I have put her there. This minute," she explained. "No longer shall she dance the First Friend."

"Ha!" said the steam-roller. "I see! She dances the First Friend too well does my Lulu, is that it? She is getting too much attention. Too much attention and not enough curtains, is that it?"

"That is it," said Stroganoff, weighing in on the side of his lieutenant. "So you go quickly and do not plague me the fuss for I am busy," he held up a hand to silence Arenskaya, "and, later, I will see to it that our good Maîtresse-de-ballet she relent."

"I relent," said Arenskaya. "She shall dance the Second Friend."

"See," said Stroganoff. "So now you go. Shoo!"

It was no doubt a remarkable thing that when Stroganoff said "Shoo!" people should go, but somehow they did.

"These six curtains," said the man with the sandy eyebrows. "They seem to be causing you a certain amount of trouble."

"You tell me," said Stroganoff. He gazed at the portrait of

Pavlova. Was there a trace of divine pity in that smile? He stood and gazed and the sandy man watched him in slight wonder.

"My friend," said Stroganoff heavily, "it seems to me at this moment that all my life has been spent with the trouble those six curtains give." He crossed to his desk, opened the cigar-box, shrugged and lit a cigarette.

"Sit down, my good friend," he said, "and I will tell about these six curtains. Make yourself comfortable," he roused himself to remember his duty as host, "for it will take all morning."

"And the rich one?" asked the sandy man.

"He can wait," said Stroganoff. "To-day I must unpack my soul."

CHAPTER III

I T begins," said Stroganoff, in St. Petersburg in 1910. . . ."

It was Sunday night. It was snowing.

At the Maryinsky Theatre the divine Trefilova was to dance the sugar plum fairy and the Imperial Court, glittering and scandalizing, had assembled to see her do it. Friends bowed cordially, enemies bowed stiffly, and creaky old generals smoked shaky cigarettes in amber holders. Everyone knew everyone else, and had done for generations. A new face was an event, a slightly distressing event—like an uninvited guest at a Christmas party.

And to-night there were two of them sitting in the front row of the dress circle, a bald-headed young man and a girl bending raptly towards each other, an island of mutual admiration in a sea of encrusted hostility.

"Voilà!" said the young man, "everything is as I have promised you. First," he tapped a well-pleased finger, "we are in St. Petersburg on our honeymoon. Second," he tapped another, "your mamoushka is in Omsk. Third, we are alone together and we are going to have the complete holiday and forget the ballet. And last (which you taunted me I could never achieve), we have the best seats at the Maryinsky!"

"Vladimir, you are wonderful," said the bride. "How did you do it?"

"Ah," said Stroganoff. "That is my secret."

It was no secret to the encrusted nobility around them. Old Godorenko had sold his seats again—though he had promised faithfully not to only five years ago. Old Godorenko would have to be spoken to. Provincials at the Maryinsky! It would be his moneylender next.

The conductor rapped with his baton on the gold stand. The house sprang, rustled and creaked to its feet. The Imperial box had filled with figures as glorious as the suns and moons of the universe, as remote as wax dolls in a shop window. Behind them was Rasputin.

"Vladimir," breathed the young bride, "imagine if it were I who dance to-night. Would I die?"

"A thousand times, my little one," whispered Stroganoff, "and because of this you would dance like all the angels there have ever been."

Light in the myriad chandeliers grew dim. Footlights glowed up, warming the curtain to its exciting crimson life. A voiceless ah! ran through the house, and Tchaikowsky's Christmas music gaily took possession of the auditorium.

The curtain went up.

"Punctual," said Vladimir Stroganoff in awe.

* * *

To arrive at the Opera House, Omsk, a dewy choryphée with an anything but dewy mamoushka, to catch the eye of the boss, to dance Raymonda, Coppélia and the Peri within six months, to marry the boss in seven, to come to the capital on your honeymoon, with mamoushka weeping and definitely left behind, and to sit in the front row of the Grand Circle of the Maryinsky, watching Trefilova, of whom one had only dreamed, dancing the familiar and yet so different Sugar Plum—it was altogether too much. Long before the end of the third act Natasha Stroganova was in tears.

She reached for her husband's hand. "Vladimir," she said, "what is the use? I shall never dance better than this."

"Mooch better," said Stroganoff absently. "Mooch, mooch better." He gazed entranced at the stage.

"But I am mad," said Natasha, pulling herself together. "Of course I will dance better. Or at least as well," she amended humbly, gazing in a mixture of joy and sorrow at the perfection of a frozen arabesque.

"Sssh," said the generals on either side of them simultaneously.

On the stage the enchantment continued, glory replaced glory, comical, vigorous, technical and all well schooled, for were they not specially chosen glories, trained for ten years in a seminary from which a nun would have fled in panic, convinced that her vocation had been nothing but a girlish fancy?

The audience appraised, whispered and applauded.

And now the ballet drew towards its brilliant close. The pas des fleurs disintegrated into separate posies, each tearing off a formidable technical variation with only a slight strain at the edge of the smile to show the concentration that was going into all this floating, and each safely accomplished passage crowned with applauding hands and knowing nods.

"That one," said Stroganoff as a girl like a frozen flame vanished into the wings, "that one has promise."

In a shower of "Brava! brava! Bis!" Pavlova came back to take her bow.

"She is good," said Natasha. She sought for some technical criticism and failed to find it. "But her soul is not yet awake."

"You are wrong, my pigeon," said Stroganoff softly. "The soul of that one will never sleep."

"Sssh," said the generals on either side of them.

"Ssh, ssh," said the general behind.

For now the finale was triumphantly achieved. Everybody on the stage was lighthearted, for soon the difficulties of the day would be over and they would be sitting, safe and relaxed, discussing the catastrophies of others over supper and not a thing to worry about till class at 9 a.m. next morning; and everybody in the auditorium a little sad because the ballet had come to an end and there would not be another performance till next Wednesday and not another gathering of such exclusive grandeur till to-day week. After all, what were two seats in the dress circle?

"Brava! brava! Bis!" cried the two seats in unison, as Trefilova took one, two, three, four curtains. And at the fifth Natasha turned to the applauding impresario beside her.

"Five curtains, Vladimir," she said. "Did you count? Five curtains."

"Pourquoi pas," said Stroganoff. He went on clapping.

"I must do better," mused Natasha Stroganova. "Vladimir," she turned starrily, "when I am Assoluta I shall have six."

"A thousand, my darling," said Stroganoff obligingly, the impresario sunk in the adoring husband.

"And that," Stroganoff told the sandy man, "was the beginning of all my troubles. For though I promise without reflecting and forget the next instant, my wife she remind me the next morning. And the morning after. And every day while we are married and long after that." He sighed.

"I made a promise once," said the sandy man reflectively. "In writing." He shook his head.

"Still," said Stroganoff fairly, "if the promise begin my troubles, it also begin my success. For, were it not for that, I would not be the great impresario, famous, powerful and rich." He stopped abruptly. "Sometimes," he added.

"Quite," said the sandy man. He smiled.

"But we are at the Maryinsky," said Stroganoff, "and presently I am arguing with General Dumka—the one who go 'Ssh!' all the time. Poor Dumka," said Stroganoff, "the last time I see him he is serving zakuski in a little Russian restaurant in Paris—but he is still in his uniform of the Russian Imperial Guard."

"Poor old boy," said the sandy man.

"Do not weep for him," said Stroganoff. "He had his memories. You would hardly credit it, my friend," he chuckled suddenly, "but to the last he maintained that Dourakova was a purer Sugar Plum than the divine Trefilova." He kissed his fingers.

"My friend," said General Dumka, "I will not argue with you. Dourakova is far, far purer." In his agitation his cigarette jabbed wide of his amber holder.

"And me, I will not argue either," said Stroganoff hotly. "But I tell you that to demand a greater purity than we have applauded to-night . . ."

"Please," said Natasha, "I would like some supper."

"Trefilova is enchanting," ceded General Dumka. "She is improving all the time," he pointed out generously. "But to compare this with the mastery of the incomparable Dourakova . . ."

"Pardon," said an old lady. Her furs brushed past the passionate little group blocking the exit.

"Please," said Natasha, "I would like some supper."

"Dourakova," said Stroganoff contemptuously. "Where in your Dourakova do you find the well-placed shoulder, the iron hips, the frozen arabesque? . . .

"And where in Trefilova," interrupted General Dumka, "do you find the fire?"

"Where," said Natasha plaintively, "can I get some supper?"

★   ★   ★

"To Dourakova," said General Dumka. He raised his glass of Mumm and drank.

"To Trefilova," said Stroganoff. He drank and plonked his glass defiantly on the table.

"To all our dear friends in Omsk," said Natasha and burst into tears.

Almire Cubat, cruising benevolently round his fashionable French-Russian restaurant, condescended to glance at the weeping lady and raised an interested yet slightly puzzled eyebrow. It was not that tears were at all unusual at the Cubat where all the ballerinas came after triumphant and other appearances—ma foi non!—but so far he had always known not only the shedder, but also precisely why she was shedding. Everyone knew a ballerina had her sorrows; the fierce rivalries, the broken contracts, the muddled love-life, the papoushka whose pupils were falling off, and the mamoushka who smiled bravely through a trail of dependent aunts—oh, it was simple enough, informed as he was, to keep track of the reasons for a ballerina's tears. But he did not know this pretty little lady, nor the chubby well-waistcoated gentleman patting her. But he knew General Dumka enough and he raised the other eyebrow at him mutely asking for an explanation.

"Madame is a little distressed," said Dumka benevolently. "She weeps because she is not yet Assoluta."

"Ah, bon," said Almire Cubat. All was clear. "My best wishes to Madame."

He bowed and drifted off to welcome a bank of roses standing in the entrance, bowed lower, found a white hand among the foliage and kissed it.

"Oh, Almire," said Trefilova, "I am so unhappy." She clutched his hand. "My variation to-night. It was like a circus girl. Oh, how could I dance like that!"

The divine Trefilova winked away a tear.

"Madame is too severe," said Almire Cubat. "The notices will contradict her."

The orchestra burst into Casse-Noisette. Trefilova felt a little sick. She smiled at the leader. She glanced across the room to a table where Valerien Svetlov, the foremost of the critics, was utilizing her twenty minutes' lateness to steep his pen in—what? She felt a little sicker. She would not know until to-morrow though she was supping with him to-night. Probably in vitriol, she reflected, as she smilingly allowed Cubat to lead her to the table, for he had given her charms no chance to soften whatever opinion he might have formed.

"Ah, there you are, my dear," said Svetlov, handing an ominous slip of paper to a courier. "Did the students chair you to the very door?"

No indication. "They did," said Trefilova. She flopped down.

The little bride, her tears dried, had followed every detail of the divine Trefilova's progress with breathless attention. Stroganoff, of course, was too busy arguing the perfections of the dancer to notice that she had arrived.

"How wonderful," thought Natasha, "to enter such a magnificent and crowded restaurant, the greatest of the great, to have the orchestra play your ballet in compliment to your appearance, to take it all so much for granted, and to sail across the room, acknowledging this one, ignoring that one, and so to sup casually with the most dreaded critic in all Russia with never a thought or care of what he might write about you to-morrow."

"You eat nothing, my dear," said Svetlov. "A little caviar."

"I am tired, Valerien," said Trefilova. "I wish to-morrow

would never come. Tell me," she nerved herself to ask the impermissible, "was I so very terrible?"

Svetlov patted her shoulder. "A little Mumm, my dear," he said.

So she had danced badly. She gulped her champagne.

"I took five curtains," she said defiantly.

"But, of course," said Svetlov. "These Maryinsky audiences . . ."

Through the restaurant progressed a broad-shouldered man. He was tall, but his tread was quiet. He bowed but he did not smile. His hair was black, but there was a white lock in it. He was Sergei Diaghilev, bearing the fruits of his first Paris triumph. Already many people in St. Petersburg were afraid of him.

With Diaghilev was a coterie of artists, all young, all enthusiastic, all men of ideas, and all trying to look as inscrutable as he did. Benois, Bakst, Fokine, Stravinsky, Nouvel and P. Puthyk.

But once seated at the table impassivity dissolved into flying hands—hands composing steps, hands executing steps, hands painting scenery, hands playing a hurdy-gurdy, hands describing moods, hands describing characters, and not a single pair of hands concerned with where the money was coming from. Somewhere, well at the back of Diaghilev's mind, was a nasty little nag, but this was not the moment for it. Not with Petroushka beginning at last to take form, a daring, realistic, iconoclastic form that would uproot dead artistic hedges and send every critic in sight doddering to his well-merited grave. They shot a look at

Svetlov. Ha! If that one knew what was coming to him!

"Never felt better in my life," Svetlov was boasting, at a happy distance from his doom. "I don't say I like Karlsbad prunes," manfully he swallowed one, "but they do help the digestion."

Trefilova smiled mistily at him over a mountain of meringues. That Conductor! She'd have a word with him to-morrow.

"Your health, Madame," said General Dumka. "And may we see you dancing in our capital soon."

"Oh," said Natasha. The idea planted itself.

"The time will come," said Stroganoff proudly. "For the moment you understand, Omsk has need of her."

"Omsk," said General Dumka. Not for the first time that evening his eyeglass fell out.

"You excuse me!" A young man had slouched over to the recovering General's elbow. "But have you by chance a hundred roubles to lend me till to-morrow?"

The General suffered a relapse.

"Or maybe," said Nicholas Nevajno, for it was none other, "till next month."

"A hundred roubles," said General Dumka weakly.

"You see," Nevajno explained, " I come here to-night and I think I am guest. But alas," he sagged, "it appears that I am host." He looked as though he were about to burst into tears.

General Dumka played for time. "Permit me to present my good friend Nicholas Nevajno," he announced. "A choreographer with a great future."

A choreographer! Stroganoff leaped to his feet.

"Sit down, my friend," he said. "Champagne," he poured. "One hundred roubles!" he felt for his wallet.

Down the restaurant pranced a dark, petite, heavily perfumed young girl, clearly a dancer, for behind, beside, and in front of her bobbed a foam of balletomane generals of the second rank of discrimination and the last legs of lechery. She was Arenskaya.

Already she was laden with jewels and orchids. Already she was plundering the props baskets. And already she wanted to dance Giselle, but Teleyakov preferred Pavlova. Unfair.

She passed by Diaghilev's table. She unleashed her personality on the preoccupied group around him. The group remained preoccupied. Infuriating creatures. All save one, whose entrechatting hand floated static in mid-air as he gazed at her. P. Puthyk.

Maybe that one wouldn't dream of his English Governess to-night!

Arenskaya pranced on. Two generals dead-heated to pull out her chair. Three more reached for her furs. The waiters were nowhere. Arenskaya shook her curls at them and turned her bird-bright attention to the company at large.

There was Trefilova weeping into her coffee. Naturally, after that performance. There was Karsavina drying her eyes—now what had she just heard? Of course—the cancelled matinée. There was Pavlova—crying buckets, that one! And there was Kyasht, blonde, dimpling, and not a tear in sight. Arenskaya pranced over.

"My darling," she said, "but you were divine, and not nearly so fat as all have been whispering. No, no." She pranced back. She stole a glance. Kyasht was weeping all right.

"Champagne," said Arenskaya well pleased.

Nicholas Nevajno had not gone back to his guests. He was drinking Stroganoff's champagne and he was talking. He was talking about his ballet that no one would put on. General Dumka had long since fallen asleep, but Stroganoff was listening entranced. What an attraction for Omsk!

And the little Natasha looked and looked at the glittering, modish, eating, drinking, singing, weeping, laughing company before her. How wonderful it all was. If only she belonged.

She wept.

CHAPTER IV

V<small>LADIMIR</small>," said Natasha, "do you love me?"

"My darling," said Stroganoff. He stretched out his night-shirted arms.

"Then," said the bride, dodging nimbly, "you will arrange that I dance in Petersburg."

"We will see," said Stroganoff, side-stepping after her. "We will see," he promised.

But Natasha buttoned up her dressing-gown and crouched over the log fire, her mouth set in a grim little line.

"My darling," said Stroganoff gently, "do not look like that. It reminds me of your mamoushka—God bless her." He put his hands on her shoulders. Natasha shook them off.

Stroganoff gazed wistfully round the bridal suite of the newest hotel in St. Petersburg. It featured red plush curtains with bobbled fringes, two sofas and a footstool, a wardrobe of immense proportions, a double bed with a new spring mattress, a great deal of gold paint almost everywhere, a painting of the Retreat of Napoleon from Moscow,* and a bathroom. There was no hot water, but it had

* We think it was Napoleon. The hat suggested it.

been promised for to-morrow for some days now. In the meantime, if you tugged the bell often enough, old Ivan would stagger in with a couple of cans, steaming—perhaps. Stroganoff fetched a deep sigh. Of what use all this luxury if his little pigeon fastened her dressing-gown.

"My little snowflake," he said. "Sois raisonable. Melt a little."

The snowflake looked reproachful. "Vladimir," she said, "sometimes I marvel at you. How can you refuse me anything at a moment like this?"

She undid a button. It was not a very important button.

"You must understand, my friend," said Stroganoff, "ça, c'était avant."

The sandy man nodded. His French was not very good, but he could follow that one.

"Vladimir," said his bride, "look at me."

Vladimir threw his hands up to the painted ceiling. "Mais voyons, ma petite," he said, "what else have I been doing for the last hour? And if you take this thing off," he tugged at the dressing-gown, "I could do it better."

"Vladimir, don't be coarse," said the bride. She crossed her arms and shielded her endangered bosom.

"What say you," suggested Stroganoff, playful but diffident, "that I pick you up in my arms like a little feather and carry you to the bed?"

"No," said the bride. "Not till you agree to present me in St. Petersburg," ultimated the ballerina's firmed mouth.

Stroganoff resigned himself. No fond endearments, however skilfully put, would change this conversation. He too put on his dressing-gown. He crossed to the samovar and brought back two tumblers of tea. He found his amber cigarette-holder and stuck a cigarette in it. Now all was set for reasoned argument.

"My darling," he said. "We are very well in Omsk. We have the Opera with the three performances a week and the many people with the season ticket so we do not care if they come or not. You are famous and my papoushka," he pointed out, "is rich and for the moment can defray the deficit."

How was he doing? But the little mouth had tightened.

"Omsk," said Natasha, "is not St. Petersburg."

"Bien sûr." A skilled debater, Stroganoff pounced on the point. "In St. Petersburg there is no new apartment, which you have so tastefully furnished and for which the papoushka does not yet know how much he has to pay. Our Louis Quinze." He kissed his fingers.

"Your papoushka," said Natasha, "is very rich. But also," she added, "he is very rude. He called my mamoushka a cow. My poor mamoushka, who has done everything for me."

"Console yourself, my darling," said Stroganoff. "He meant only that the cow is the mother of the graceful little calf."

"Ha!" said Natasha, "you cannot fool me, Vladimir. I do not believe that you love my mamoushka either."

Stroganoff made to change the subject.

"In Omsk," he said, "we stage all the great ballets and where else can you dance Giselle?"

"In St. Petersburg," said Natasha.

"Ha," said Stroganoff vexed, "so now she persuades Pavlova to abdicate! Proceed, my pigeon. I will watch you with interest." He folded his arms.

His little pigeon pummelled his chest. "You are a brute, Vladimir Stroganoff," she said, "a tyrant, a boor! And a drunkard," she added for luck. "And why you have not yet beaten me I cannot understand."

"Me neither," said Stroganoff mildly.

"You give me my company, yes. But where? In Omsk!" She shuddered. "In Omsk, where nobody knows anything. Who comes to Omsk?" she demanded.

"Nicholas Nevajno," said Stroganoff. "Already I have pay him the advance in salary. I keep this as a surprise for you, my little pigeon."

Natasha waved the surprise aside.

"Vladimir Stroganoff," she said, "you bring me to Petersburg with my company, and with my mamoushka and," she remembered something, "my six curtains or else . . ."

"My friend," said Stroganoff, "I was very rash. But also," he gazed unseeingly out over Covent Garden, "it was my honeymoon. So I promised."

"Quite," said the sandy man.

"But that night Natasha was tired from her victory," said Stroganoff. "So . . ." He sighed.

CHAPTER V

V LADIMIR," said Natasha, "do you love me?"

"Toujours," said Stroganoff, with wariness.

An unusual emotion for a honeymooning husband when this particular question crops up. But Stroganoff was lying in the upper berth of a railway compartment and Natasha was in the lower berth so the question could not be an overture to a delightful interlude but merely the prelude to some less delightful demand.

"Vladimir," said Natasha, "you have promised to speak to your father."

"As soon as we get to Omsk," said Stroganoff. He dangled his hand into the darkness. A small hand came snuggling into it. One more little hint and he would be clambering down.

"Six curtains," breathed the bride.

"Go to sleep," said the husband, fed up.

The Passenger-Postal Train chugged its way serenely towards Omsk. It had been chugging for four days now and it had still quite a long way to go, and was in no hurry to get there. It stopped for water, it stopped for fuel, it stopped for flowers, and it stopped for luck, it might even stop for a signal if the engine-driver happened to notice it, but in the main it stopped for food. The mail must go through— but in those days, it didn't have to go through so very quickly, the ordinary Russian being only too gratified to receive a letter at all to worry about the time it had taken to reach him. And while the mail progressed, passengers had to eat. All the villagers en route were well aware of this and ran to the station with hopefully cooked chickens every day in the hope that this would be the one on which the train would arrive. And sometimes it did. It was usually the previous train. But the passengers were always hungry.

In the larger villages they were more ambitious. There would be an inn with hot bortsch and pirojki, great joints and pigs roasted whole. Dining at a stationary table, with the light of a log fire playing over the walls and warding off the home-made baskets the peasants were trying to sell, made a delightful break in the journey. The engine-driver, who liked a good meal himself and a little singing afterwards, thoughtfully allowed plenty of time for it. And his tenor ringing out under the rafters sounded fine and the bass of the liberal gentleman with the looking-down-the-nose bride—what there was of it—blended pleasingly in Gayda Troika if a little less well in the Two Guitars. So pleased had the bass been with their singing that he had promised the engine-driver seats for the ballet whenever he came to Omsk. The engine-driver was wondering if he could hold the train there overnight. He couldn't see why not.

"Vladimir," said the bride into the night, "are you asleep?"

"I was," said Stroganoff.

"I have been thinking," said Natasha. "If I am to have my company in Petersburg this year as you have promised, it is essential that you speak to the papoushka at once."

"As soon as we get to Omsk," said Stroganoff in his sleep.

For that had been the question which, like the chimes of the churches had punctuated the days and the nights of the honeymoon. The carillon had been heard at all the most expensive places and at the most unexpected moments. At Fabergé, choosing the gold and turquoise tea-set which was to make all Omsk envious so that papoushka could not afford to send it back. At the Parfumerie and the Pastry Cook's. Crossing the Nevsky Prospekt. In the middle of "A Life for the Tzar." First thing in the morning, last thing at night, and twice while cabling papoushka for more funds. How often was the good old one in the minds of his children and every time his image, usually a wincing one, floated before their eyes, Natasha was reminded of the all-important matter her husband would have to take up with him on their return. For, before Stroganoff could present her in St. Petersburg, the papoushka would have to find the finance.

"Vladimir," the little voice cooed anxiously into the darkness. "Vladimir," it cooed a little more sharply.

"Yes, my little goose," said Stroganoff, jerked out of Trefilova's triumphant appearance in Omsk with Pavlova begging him to arrange one for her and General Dumka unaccountably asleep in the dress circle. "Yes, my little snowbird—what is it? You would like some water?" And he prepared to heave himself out, if not with alacrity, at least with an appearance of willingness.

"Vladimir," said the bride, "I know you have promised, but promise me that you will speak to the papoushka as you have promised."

"As soon as we get to Omsk," said Stroganoff and pulled the blankets over his head.

CHAPTER VI

IT was Omsk.

It was four weeks later.

"Vladimir," said Natasha, "promise me something . . ."

She was in her dressing-room, the star's dressing-room, gazing critically into her mirror, while a bent-double black behind, which was all you could see of mamoushka, stitched the ribbons of her ballet shoes—no chances were to be taken to-night.

For Natasha was dancing Giselle for the first time, and the Opera House was crowded—well, fairly full.

"Now do not unquiet yourself," said Stroganoff. "Relax the nerves, my darling. You will have the success triumphant. At the rehearsal to-day you are unsurpassable," said the impresario. "And also," said the husband, "you are delicious."

He kissed her cheek. The mamoushka unbent herself, put the wreath straight, glared at Stroganoff and returned to her shoes.

"Vladimir," said Giselle, "promise me something . . ."

"Yes, my little angel," said Stroganoff fondly.

"Promise me you will speak to papoushka. . . ."

Affection vanished.

"As soon as the performance is over," said Stroganoff.

In the auditorium of the Opera House the lights went down. The conductor mounted his rostrum. He bowed to a large watch-chained stomach in the stage-box. The stomach inclined itself.

Aliosha Stroganoff never missed a performance of his ballet. Neither did his banker. But their reasons were different. Stroganoff, merchant, loved art and he loved his son —his only son—and now his dream had come true and the latter was presenting him with the first. But the banker loved Aliosha, and he was there to see his crack-brained young son didn't ruin him.

"Seven hundred roubles in the house," he said. "Hardly enough to cover the salaries."

Aliosha smiled at him. "Abram, Abram," he shook a playful finger and his stomach heaved a little, "here is my daughter-in-law dancing Giselle for the first time and," he pointed out, "my um . . . discovery dancing the Queen of the Wilis and you talk to me about money. No, no, Abram— it is not the moment." And he gazed expectantly at the villagers gathered outside Giselle's cottage.

"It is never the moment not to talk about money," said the banker shocked.

"Sssh—there she is, my Katusha," said Aliosha. He gazed enamoured at the stage. "Third from the left in the back row. Charming—no?" He patted his stomach. "And she dances well too," he said loyally. "In the second act she has her variation. The mother of my daughter-in-law did not wish it, but I was firm."

"Ah, that one," said the banker darkly.

The performance went on. Giselle emerged from her cottage, all blushes and palpitations. In the wings mamoushka was having palpitations too. But the House took kindly to Natasha. She was young, she was pretty to look at, her pointes were not very strong, but what would you, you could not expect an Egorova at Omsk. But as for the Prince! Were there not less knowledgeable cities? Vladivostok, for example. Why didn't he go there?

"That one," said the banker disparagingly as the Prince leapt, but not very high, into the air, "that one," he repeated, "is no Nijinsky."

The dancer who was no Nijinsky came down again. He looked round for the ballerina. He managed to catch up with her.

"He is no Nijinsky," agreed Aliosha, "but he is the second-best Vint player in Omsk." He patted his stomach.

"And that reminds me," said the banker, "must you play so high?"

Vladimir Stroganoff dashed into the box. "She is superb —no? You are happy, yes?" He dashed out again.

"When I was young," said Aliosha fondly, "I, too, ran about like a zany."

"And now that you are older," said the banker, "you sit still, but you are no wiser. Discovery! At your age!"

"Abram, you are jealous," said Aliosha. "And also you are getting past it. For one thing," he said, gazing critically at the much smaller stomach, "you are too fat." He clasped his hands over his own.

The banker grinned into his beard. That was all Aliosha

knew. He thought comfortably of his Saturday nights. Past it—ha!

The ballet creaked on. The Princess arrived with her customary thirst. Giselle's scolding old Mother, not so different from the one in the wings, at the moment rehearsing what she was going to say to the conductor later, helped to slake it. Gratified, the Princess bestowed some pearls on Giselle. Overjoyed Giselle danced.

"Oh, my darling," moaned the mamoushka in the wings. She went on crossing herself for the next three minutes.

"She dances like a goddess," said Vladimir Stroganoff, pausing to snatch a peep between his many errands. He rushed away to collect the laurel wreath due to be presented later—it always was—to the man who was no Nijinsky.

It was the interval. The Safety Curtain came trundling down. It was not fireproof, but it carried advertisements. And here were all the advertisers in the stalls gazing raptly at it. The hairdresser, the couturier, the jeweller, the brothel-keeper (Chez Planchette, Massage), and the Best Tailor in Omsk—he said so.

"And he is right," said Aliosha. He patted his waistcoat.

"Rabinovitch," said the banker, "is half the price and just as good." Defiantly he flicked a speck of dust off his sleeve.

"My son," said Aliosha proudly, "had six suits and two overcoats made for him in St. Petersburg."

"Aie!" said the banker.

"He trembles to tell me," said Aliosha, "and I shall be very angry and nearly ruined when he does. But in the meantime," he grinned, "I have peered into his cupboard. The cloth." He kissed his fingers.

But not everybody in the house was advertising on the Safety Curtain and not everybody was scrimmaging at the Kvass Counter. Some were returning from it. And in the Foyer the sole topic of conversation was the new Giselle, with Petkov, the local critic, strong on Tannhäuser but weak on the Ballet, listening-in to as many places as he could manage.

La Stroganova was bewitching, enchanting, and could have been worse. Her variations had great appeal and not enough strength. Her mad scene was poignant, and enough to make a cow laugh. A finished performance and too immature. What would you—to see Pavlova you had to go to Petersburg. The Management were to be congratulated, and they ought never to have let her go on. A true ballerina in the making, and she would never make a ballerina.

Baffled, the critic withdrew to the Kvass Counter. Oh, for the space to put it all down and let his readers decide for themselves!

But in the wings opinion, dressed in the evanescences of Act II, was more unanimous. A crowd of dancers were warmly surrounding Natasha, a band of good old troopers, long past any hope for themselves save that of getting by, rejoicing in the triumph of a newcomer.

"You were exquisite."

"You were superb."

"You made me cry."

A woodcutter came up. He had been woodcutter to many

a Giselle, the Prince's first companion in many a Swan Lake and Burgomaster to countless Coppélias.

"My dear," said Kashkavar Jones, "I am very happy for you." He wept.

"You were better than Preobrajenskaya," said Aliosha's Discovery. "Much," she convinced herself.

"Mind my lilies," said the man who was no Nijinsky.

A little way off a crowd of mamoushkas were surrounding Natasha's mamoushka, a band of tried old troopers, past any hope for their daughters save that of getting a rise in salary or promotion from the third row to the second, and they were rejoicing, after their manner, in the triumph of a newcomer.

"She looked very pretty—no one can take that from her."

"Her hair was nice—if you like it that way."

"Only five mistakes—I counted them."

"I have seen worse Giselles—I think."

"How clever you were," said a mamoushka, who, though sorely tried, had been saving this up for weeks, "to marry her to Monsieur le Directeur."

"I thank you," said Natasha's mamoushka grimly. She could take a lot of this with her daughter queening it. "And also please thank from me your own daughters for supporting as best they can my little genius."

She waddled off with the bridal veil. Honour was satisfied. The impertinence of these dancers' mothers, she thought, as she placed the bridal veil over her daughter's tingling head. Their clumsy daughters would never get to Petersburg. Why, if she'd only had a mamoushka like herself, she might have danced in Petersburg too in her time. Nijni-Novgorod! Pfui!

Presently, after the twenty-minute interval had lasted but three-quarters of an hour, Act II began.

"Now," said Aliosha, as the Queen of the Wilis came plodding on, "now you will see something." And he leant forward, screening the stage from the banker. "My Discovery," he gloated, as Queen of the Wilis disentangled her veil from the gravestone.

"She doesn't dance very well," said the banker, peering over Aliosha's shoulder.

"She is very pretty," said Aliosha sensibly, "no one can take that from her."

"And," said the banker, nearly nasty, "she has had the sense to prefer the rich father."

"And why not?" said Aliosha. "At my age I do not expect them to love me. When they did, it was not restful." He patted his stomach.

"Aliosha, you are a wicked old man," said the banker.

"Yes, yes," said Aliosha, delighted.

Nicholas Nevajno, choreographer of the future, came slouching into the box, pushed forward a chair, sat down in front of the banker, and watched the stage critically for some moments.

"Pfui!" he said.

Aliosha bridled. "Sir," he accused, "you spit you of my Discovery?"

"Did you discover this?" said Nevajno incredulously. "Where?"

Aliosha blushed.

"That is his business," said the banker, quickly.

"Ah, ça," said Nevajno. "As to that I offer no opinion. But for the ballet—pfui!"

Giselle arose from the grave. She floated in the arms of her betrayer. Her partner did his best to float with her, but he was no Nijinsky. The banker wept a little.

"Pfui," said Nevajno, "this is not art. It is but the sticky sentiment. Coralli!" He spat.

The banker blew his nose. He looked at Nevajno with disfavour. He remembered something.

"Young man," he said coldly, "your account at my bank is overdrawn."

Nevajno considered this. "You mean I have no money," he said acutely.

"Not a kopeck," said the banker. "So don't write any more cheques for they won't be met."

Nevajno considered again. He saw an objection.

"But," he pointed out, "the people to whom I give my scheques give me money for them."

"That," said the banker grimly, "is their affair."

"So," said Nevajno. He brightened. "But this is good news," he said. "Then," he sought to get it quite clear, "while I have no money in the bank you pay nothing on my scheques to the people who give me money for them."

"Not a kopeck," said the banker. "Quite bluntly, Mr. Nevajno, they will bounce."

"You promise," said Nevajno anxiously.

"I promise," said the banker. "They will bounce," he repeated grimly.

50

"But this is terrific," Nevajno shook him warmly by the hand. "This concept of yours—it is colossal. Never, never will I be able to thank you."

And the banker watched in horror as Nevajno turned to Aliosha, pulled out a cheque book and whispered something. Without taking his eyes off the stage where Katusha was denying the betrayer salvation, Aliosha slid his hand deep into his pocket, pulled out a golden rouble-purse and thumbed out a handful of coins.

"Aie!" said the banker.

Nevajno smiled at him. "It works," he confided. "He has schange me a schmall scheque."

In a dream of bliss he wandered out.

On the stage Giselle was borne back to her grave. . . .

. . . "Ah the emotions of that Giselle," Stroganoff gazed raptly at the ceiling. "The packed house. The cheering audience. The enthusiastic critics. And me, I am everywhere and my heart is in my mouth, and all the time I am talking, talking, talking."

"Sure," said the sandy man.

"For in those days, you must understand I am young and hoping," said Stroganoff. "Ah, the things that hang on those hopes. I had not then the pessimism that you see with me to-day, my friend." He shook his head and sighed heavily. "For what have I to look for now? Only the worries and the exasperation. If all go well it is the artists' talent, if bad, it is the fault of the management. And also," he faced it, "there is the finance. Always the finance." He sagged.

"There is the rich one," said the sandy man tentatively.

"That one!" said Stroganoff. "He will be fat and bloated and already he will be complaining. Also he will ask me many questions, and all about money. Every time I spend the sou he will look at the books, and," past experience shot up, "complain of the handwriting. You will see, my friend," he prophesied, "the rich one will come into this office as though already it belongs to him, he will ask me why I do not present the comedy musical, he will talk all the time about himself, and also he will have a little friend, whom his wife has not met, and for whom I must find the small solo—say the Prelude in Sylphides."

The sandy man put his hand over his mouth.

"And even if he give me all the moneys I need," said Stroganoff, "what is there new that I can do with them? I can take a bigger theatre." He dismissed it. "I can engage Markova, Dolin, Danilova and Franklin." He waved them away. "With them, and possibly," he considered, "Robert Helpmann, I could go to Covent Garden and," he brightened, "what is more, I could fill it. And after this triumph," he wagged a finger, "I go straight to the Metropolitan, New York. You shall see I am at the Metropolitan in the fall." He thought of something else. "Tell me, my friend," he said earnestly, "with what ballet do you think we should open?"

"Er," said the sandy man. . . .

CHAPTER VII

"Oof," said Stroganoff. He looked round. His little love-nest bore the air of a room that had held far too many people in it far too long.

Smoke draped the ceiling, deflated cushions littered the floor, the Fabergé tea-set, brought in triumphantly assembled, was now scattered, nicotine ended all over the place—and one less at that (how Little Igor had blushed!), and—Mon Dieu! there was a burn on one of the Louis Quinze fauteuils. Fortunately Natasha had not yet seen.

Stroganoff sat down hurriedly. Maybe with a needle and thread? Or maybe not! He sighed.

Natasha's first-night party was over at last. Stroganoff had invited almost the entire company and the others had come, anyway. Those who could not crowd into the drawing-room had peered round the door of the passage and had vodka and zakuski passed to them in a flurry of "pardons." Anyway, not many of the gowns were permanently ruined.

It had been a triumph and toast after toast had been drunk to the heroine of the occasion. Almost she might have been Kshessinskaya.

"To your four curtains, my darling," said Stroganoff. "No

one in Omsk has taken more. Save," he remembered, "the cousin of Chaliapin."

They drank.

"When I am in St. Petersburg," said Natasha distinctly, "I shall have six."

Aliosha looked up.

"To the papoushka," cried Stroganoff quickly. "Let us drink to the papoushka."

They drank.

Then Kashkavar Jones had made a speech, and though it was inaudible, Little Igor nodded agreement. The man who was no Nijinsky left early, Nevajno did not come at all and the mamoushka had fallen asleep in the kitchen. But the rest had lingered on for two hours after making their final farewells and had started to talk politics, which meant that they would not go at all, and the papoushka was yawning his head off, and Natasha was nudging her husband in the ribs—each time a little more sharply, and something drastic would have to be done.

So Stroganoff said "Shoo!"

Now they were all gone. Stroganoff had seen them into their droshkys and waved them good-bye, and exploded back at the neighbours and come in and closed the door.

"Oof," he said, and sat down quickly on the burn.

But Natasha was not noticing. She had savoured her triumph, and now it was time to think of the future.

"Vladimir," she pointed to the stomach rising and falling in front of the fire. "Now is the moment."

Stroganoff backed a little. "But no. Papoushka is tired. See how he slumbers. To-morrow, my little pigeon."

"To-night," said Natasha grimly.

"But my little one," said Stroganoff, "let us be kind and also tactful. It is not the subject with which to wake the sleeping father."

A log fell out of the fire. The sleeping father blinked awake and heaved himself to his feet.

"It is the time that I was in bed," he said. "And you, too, my children. Where," he demanded, "is my Katusha?" He looked round.

"She has gone home long ago," said Natasha. "And Vladimir wishes to speak to you." She pushed him back into the chair. "Here is a nice glass of tea. Drink it and listen to Vladimir. It is very important."

But Aliosha shook his head. "It is already half-past five," he said. "When I was Vladimir's age and like him married but two months, I did not wish to sit up talking to my papoushka, may he be spared to us for many years yet. Oh, no. A papoushka," said Aliosha, "is all very well in his place, but this is not the love-nest of the new married couple when the dawn is coming. Ah, no." He wagged a finger. "I remember one night on my honeymoon . . ."

"Good night, papa," said Natasha. "Listen to Vladimir." She kissed him and withdrew.

Stroganoff tugged at his tie.

"Papa," he said. He gulped. "I have a little scheme for making the fortune colossal."

"Aie," said the Papa. "And at such an hour."

"Papoushka," said Stroganoff seriously, "you have given me much. You have given me," he started on the lowest rung, "the first-class education. The theatre of my own," he ticked it off. "My wife, my home . . ."

"And the Fabergé tea-set," said Aliosha. "The bill came only yesterday. Aie!"

"I am grateful," said Stroganoff, ignoring this, "and now I wish to pay back all the moneys that you have spent on me."

Late though the hour was, Aliosha looked startled.

"My son," he said, "did I hear you aright?"

"I wish to pay you back," said Stroganoff clearly and loudly. "But this," he made his point, "I cannot do in Omsk."

"Oho!" said Aliosha. He could not see yet where he was being led, but his instinct was warning him that he wouldn't like it.

"In Omsk there is no scope for an artist," said Stroganoff. "The Opera House," he pointed out, "has a deficit."

"This I know," said Aliosha.

"You have given me a splendid company," said Stroganoff. "And a prima ballerina!" He kissed his fingers. "But here in Omsk there is no audience that is worthy of them. So let us, my papoushka, take them to a place where there is one that will be."

"Nijni-Novgorod?" asked Aliosha.

"Nijni-Novgorod, pfui!" said Stroganoff. "There is in all the Russias only one city worthy of my company and my Natasha."

"Nu?" asked Aliosha.

"St. Petersburg," said Stroganoff.

"Aie!" said Aliosha.

The Stroganoffs mopped their brows.

"Come, my papoushka," pleaded the son, "let us look at

this with logic. We have the company superb on which you have spent much moneys. But we also have the town that cannot give it back to you. What then, is the logic?"

"To disband the company," said the papoushka.

"No," said Stroganoff, "to take it to another town. To St. Petersburg. Nevajno," he sought to clinch it, "Nevajno is stifled in Omsk."

"Ah, bon," said Aliosha.

Stroganoff tried the personal angle. "Natasha," he said, "has too much talent to waste in the Provinces. And also," he admitted, "she gives me no peace."

"Abram gives me no peace either," said Aliosha. "And what would he say if . . ."

"But, papoushka," pleaded Stroganoff, "do you not wish to see your son in St. Petersburg?"

"No," said papoushka.

"The centre of all fashion," said Stroganoff. "My Natasha the Succès fou and Kshessinskaya broken-hearted. Yourself in a box with a duchess—a grand-duchess."

Papoushka tilted his head and pondered the image. He snapped it back into position.

"Do you think," he coined a phrase, "that I am made of roubles? No and no and no!" he thundered.

*   *   *

"Come here, my darling!" A pair of sleepy white arms raised themselves from the depths of the roomy four-poster and definitely beckoned.

Regretting vaguely that he was not already in his night-shirt and pushing to the back of his mind the uncomfortable news he carried, Stroganoff advanced towards the bed, bent his head, and allowed the white arms to twine themselves around it. Tiens! they were not so sleepy after all.

"You are the best husband in the world," said Natasha. "And also the cleverest impresario."

"Entendu," said Stroganoff. "Entendu." He kissed her. Maybe he could turn her mind to something else.

"My darling," said Natasha, "you have spoken to papoushka?"

"Yes, my darling, I have spoken," said Stroganoff. Very tentatively he fondled.

Natasha snuggled up. "Then it is settled?" she asked.

"It is settled," said Stroganoff. "There is no doubt of that."

The white arms tightened their grip. "St. Petersburg," breathed Natasha. "Six curtains."

Stroganoff snuggled. He had had an idea. Let her be happy this one night—and himself too. To-morrow he would tell her the bad news before the déjeuner—or maybe after.

"But," said Stroganoff to the sandy man, "at the déjeuner my little bride was so happy that I had not the heart to spoil her mood. Besides," he nodded wisely, "it is certain that she would have slapped my face." He looked at Pavlova's portrait. He beamed. "Do you know," he said proudly, "that Pavlova, too, once give me the giffle." He rubbed his cheek tenderly.

"You amaze me," said the sandy man.

"Mon vieux," said Stroganoff with satisfaction, "there is

not in the whole of the Ballet an impresario who is more giffled than me. You must understand," he explained, "that I am to the Ballet like a father, always I try that my company are one big happy family. And what happens in a happy family when something goes wrong—poof—the happy family it giffle the papoushka."

The door opened. A small figure strode in. White with rage she stood over Stroganoff.

"Second Friend," she said. "Pfui!" She slapped his face and strode out.

"Voilà," said Stroganoff unmoved. He rubbed his cheek and resumed. "So," he said, "I did not tell my Natasha the bad news at déjeuner. And I did not tell her at tea. And I did not tell her that night. And by next morning it was no longer necessary for my papoushka had gone to see Abram the banker."

"No and no and no," said Abram the banker. His firmness was unshakeable. "Aliosha, I cannot permit that you ruin yourself."

Aliosha looked sulky. "It is my money, Abram," he said, "and if I choose to make the legitimate speculation that is my business."

The banker tried a new angle. "Aliosha," he said, "you are getting old. What pleasure is there for you to sit in a grand box with a duchess?"

"A box with a grand-duchess," corrected Aliosha crossly. "Besides, it is not the social angle that counts with me, though, mind you," he admitted, "I have never kissed the hand of a grand-duchess, but the success of my son and his little wife. And also my Katusha," he remembered. "Can I, his father, deny him this chance?"

"I insist on it," said the banker, "if this son of yours cannot make money in Omsk, how can he succeed in St. Petersburg?"

"Omsk," said Aliosha, "is a small town and has but little culture."

"Omsk," said the banker, "is the most progressive town in all the Russias." He shot his cuffs. "Have we not installed water pumps in all the side streets?" he challenged. "Are we not," he boasted, "to have the tramway soon? And it is even expected that there will be more than one tram!"

The ancient cashier shuffled in, tended a slip to the banker and whispered.

"Bounce it," said the banker tersely.

The ancient cashier shuffled out, shaking his head.

"Nevajno," said Aliosha, as though reminded of something, "is stifled in Omsk."

The banker said he was pleased to hear it.

"Abram," wheedled Aliosha, "relent. Give me back my money."

"No and no and no," said the banker.

Aliosha Stroganoff drew himself up. "Very well then," he said stiffly, "I shall go to my father." He waddled out. He remembered something. He put his head round the door.

"May he live many years yet," he said piously.

Moysha Stroganoff was ninety-one. When you looked at him you realized this at once. He spent his days in an arm-

chair snoozing in front of the fire and his thoughts ranged
vaguely round all the people who had owed him money
many years ago—for that had been his profession—and had
not paid him back—which had still not been his ruin.

For Moysha Stroganoff had been one of the moneylenders
at the Court of St. Petersburg and had done so well that
practically the whole of it was in his debt. In fact, so many
well-bred people were so deeply in his debt that little
groups of them might be seen in salons confiding in one another and speculating what to do about it. And when that
happens there is only one thing for a moneylender on the
fringes of the Court of St. Petersburg to do. It is to go somewhere else. Moysha Stroganoff knew it. He went to Omsk.
And there he had lived ever since. He and his son, and his
son's son.

A devoted family, the Stroganoffs.

"But, papoushka," said Aliosha pleadingly. "Listen a
little. Put aside your knitting and listen."

"My son, I am too old to listen," said Moysha. "And what
can you have to say, my son, that I have not already heard
many times? Besides, you mutter." He dangled a mass of
red wool. "See," he said, "a sock for my son's son's son—
when he has one."

Aliosha made the little joke. "Will he then have only one
foot?"

"My son, you are a fool," said Moysha. "And also you
have too much stomach. When I was but sixty-three I did
not have a stomach. Nor have I yet." He rapped shaky
fingers on the assortment of bones that were his diaphragm.

"And that reminds me," he said, "I am thirsty." He tinkled a bell.

"Papoushka," said Aliosha, "when you were sixty-three you had a young, clever, loving son. Me," he reminded him. "When I came to you for money to begin business you gave it. You grumbled a little, but you gave it. And now," he pointed out, "I am richer than you."

"Ah," said Moysha, "but you have not as much monies as others owe me." He looked wistfully at the files stacked in the corner. "One day," he dreamed, "I will go back to Petersburg and collect."

"Papoushka," said Aliosha, "listen to me."

"No, I am too old to listen," said Moysha firmly. "Besides, I know it already. For was not old Vanka from the bank here last night to play chess? He beat me," he said indignantly. "And that reminds me—why you schange the schmall scheque for the mad artist from Petersburg?"

"But, papa," said Aliosha.

"It is not the action of a son of mine," said Moysha reprovingly. "The bad scheque from the aristocracy—yes, that is the legitimate speculation. But not for the artist. Where," he demanded, "is the screw to turn?"

Aliosha changed the subject. "Then if you know all," he said, "you will approve, and," he raised his voice, "you will help me."

"Speak up," snapped Moysha. "Can't hear a word you say."

"You will help me," said Aliosha loudly.

"Out with it, son," said Moysha. "However disgraceful it may be," he brought in an echo from the past.

Aliosha produced a gold pencil. He opened his note-book. He wrote, "Will you find the finance to send Vladimir's ballet to St. Petersburg and my Katusha." On second thought he crossed the second item out.

The old man put on spectacles. He held the note-book upside down.

"Do you think that I am made of roubles," he demanded. "No and no and no," he trebled. "And no," he added to clinch it.

"And after this," said Stroganoff to the sandy man, "it will be clear to you, my friend, that now all is agreed and that soon we will be on our way to St. Petersburg."

The sandy man scratched his head.

CHAPTER VIII

THE love-nest was a sea of underwear, thick woollen underwear of the finest quality, all of it new. For to-morrow morning Vladimir Stroganoff was leaving for St. Petersburg to make the arrangements for the transfer of his company and when he had finished packing, he was going to have an early night to be fresh for the journey.

Natasha was helping Stroganoff to pack, and Aliosha from an armchair was giving his children moral support, while Nicholas Nevajno, who had dropped in to say good-bye, had been seized with the idea colossal for a ballet in the middle of it, and sat by the fire brooding on the details and speaking from time to time to report his progress.

"Vladimir," reminded Aliosha reprovingly, "the folding photo of your wife. You would not travel without that, my son?"

Stroganoff whipped it up and stowed it in his dressing-case. That made the fifth photograph of Natasha to be transported with him. Packing for the trip should have been a simple affair, for Stroganoff's heavy luggage was to follow with the company. All that he needed, poof!—it go into a handbag! But somehow the handbag had not been large enough. For one thing it would not hold the spare fur collar that he so clearly required, not his second-best dressing-gown, nor his bath-sheet, nor his bedroom slippers, nor the extra shirts in case the train was late or the laundry slow or the company delayed or, which was quite probable, all three. This last thought immediately suggested the need for several further articles.

"The brown suit is not enough," said Stroganoff. "Petersburg must not think I have but what I wear. And also for the evenings," he pointed out, "there is the grand tenue—with the carnation." He patted his lapel. "My pigeon, pack me my tails, my smoking, my dark grey suit with the white stripe, and also my dark blue suit with the red stripe."

"My son," said Aliosha, "these beautiful new suits for which I have paid many hundreds of roubles, in the valise they will be creased."

"You are silly, my papoushka," said Natasha. "We will put them in the trunk."

"The two trunks," corrected Stroganoff. He trundled them out, opened them, and blew.

Nevajno sneezed.

"And now," said Stroganoff a crowded half hour later, "we come to something very important. What shall I read in the hotel?"

"Read?" said Aliosha suspiciously.

"But voyons," said Stroganoff, "since my little pigeon will not be with me, would you wish that I lie and look at the ceiling?"

"You could think of me," said Natasha petulantly.

"That also," said Stroganoff. "But it is the opportunity

unique for me to read my Shakespeare in German." He picked it up, blew on it, and edged it into one of the trunks. He lowered the lid. He pressed. He pressed harder. He sat down on it.

"This ballet," said Nicholas Nevajno into the puffing and blowing, "is called Paradise."

Natasha looked at her ruby-studded watch-brooch.

"It is late," she decided, "we will close the trunks to-morrow."

"How wise you are, my pigeon," said Stroganoff. "For if I closed it now I would surely have to open it to-morrow to put in something I have not yet remembered." He kissed her. "And now, good night, little father. It is but two o'clock," he beamed. "Nice and early."

The door opened. Kashkavar Jones came in.

"I have come to wish you bon voyage, Vladimir," he said. "I had meant to come early, but in the café they were talking of the revolution, and I talk, too."

"For myself I do not believe it will come," said Aliosha. "The rich," he waved his hands largely, "will not hear of it."

"You will hear of it," said Kashkavar Jones cheerfully, "and if not, then your son will hear of it. If you read *Das Kapital* you will be convinced." He pulled it out.

The apartment panicked. All save Nicholas Nevajno, who went on brooding.

"Put it away," said Aliosha urgently. "Hide it. Tear it up. Do you not know," he said, "that if it is seen with you, you will be sent to Siberia and then you could not come with us to Petersburg? And you want to come to Petersburg," he coaxed.

Natasha and Stroganoff exchanged glances.

Kashkavar Jones looked torn. He muttered something about the glorious revolution.

"Reflect," urged Aliosha. "The revolution will be with us always. It has been with me since I was fifteen. But the chance to go to Petersburg it happen only once."

"The décor," said Nevajno, "is very difficult. For you understand that it must not look like any heaven that anyone has ever seen and yet," he shook his head, "it must look like heaven." He went back to his brooding.

Kashkavar Jones stowed his book away. "Olright," he said, "I will hide it in the cellar until we return." He shook a sorrowful head. "It is a pity, mind you, for all the time that I am in Petersburg, I shall be wondering how it ends."

After he had gone Stroganoff sighed heavily.

"Poor Kashka," he said. "I have not yet had the heart to tell him that he does not come with us."

Aliosha sat up. "Quoi donc!" he said. "Who does not come?"

"Kashkavar Jones!" said Natasha clearly. "His lifts!" She shuddered.

"Kashkavar Jones!" said Aliosha. "Not going! My son, you cannot do this thing."

The son looked sheepish. "But, papa," he said, "he is such a bad dancer."

"What do I care for that!" roared Aliosha. "Was not his mother your English governess?"

"Si," said Natasha, "and it show in his dancing."

"Clouds," said Nicholas Nevajno. "Many clouds. Some of them large." He illustrated. "And some larger."

"In St. Petersburg," said Natasha, "I must only have the best."

"Entendu," said Stroganoff with dignity. "My company it must be without flaw. And that," he pointed out, "is why we cannot take Kashka. It breaks the heart, but what would you?"

Aliosha shook a sad head. "My son, my son," he sighed, "how little you have lived. Good dancing is not everything —no, not even in the ballet. There is also the affection family. To leave behind our Kashka, who has danced for you since the first performance—we will not dwell on how—is no act of a son of mine. No." He folded his arms.

"It is expensive to take the ballet to Petersburg," argued Natasha, "and our budget it does not include the bad dancers."

"Budget—poof!" said Aliosha. "Have you no heart, woman? Imagine to yourself poor Kashka, who has pulled Vladimir's hair when he was small and whom I have many times chased with a stick from my flower-bed, left here in Omsk without his comrades and with no one from whom to borrow any money to pay his landlady." He blew his nose violently.

"Do not cry, papoushka," said Stroganoff, who was very red himself. "You have convinced me. Kashka comes with us."

"Twelve yards of tissue," said Nevajno. He seemed pleased with this remark.

"It is outrageous, this," said Natasha. "First I have to argue with Vladimir and then I have to argue with his father. Or else I am surrounded in Petersburg by all the bad dancers."

"Only Kashka," said Aliosha. "You do not understand, my daughter. If it were only a matter of dance then our Kashka would not even be in Omsk."

"As I have told you many times, my pigeon," said Vladimir, "his mother was my English governess. That is how I talk it so good." He smirked.

"And his father?" asked Natasha sharply.

"That is not known," said Aliosha. He looked the other way. He blushed.

"No golden gates," said Nevajno firmly.

Natasha threw in her hand. "Very well," she said. "Kashkavar Jones can come."

"Darling," said Vladimir overjoyed. He kissed her.

But Aliosha was still not satisfied. "And who else, Vladimir," he said ominously, "does not come to Petersburg with you?"

Vladimir Stroganoff looked distressed. But Natasha spoke out.

"Alexis," she said, "is no Nijinsky. And what is more he did not grow up in your backyard."

"You cannot blame him for that," said Aliosha. "And you have to admit, my daughter, that he tries very hard. And also," he pointed out, "I have lent him a hundred roubles on the security of his salary. Make a note, Vladimir," he enjoined, "to pay it to me."

"No," said Natasha. She stamped her foot.

The door opened. The man who was no Nijinsky came in. He was wearing a bright mustard overcoat.

"What say you?" he preened himself. "I had it made special for St. Petersburg."

"A sunset," said Nevajno. "Amber and surprise pink. And after that the deluge." He went back to his brooding.

"My friend," said Stroganoff, "I plan for the early night, and," he pointed out, "it is already three o'clock. Is this the time to ask me to admire overcoats? Mark you," he said judiciously, "it is a pretty colour, but it is too tight round the shoulders."

"I go to the tailor at once," said the man who was no Nijinsky, alarmed. He looked at the clock. "I still go," he said defiantly. "I cannot appear in Petersburg with the too tight coat."

He went.

Aliosha roared with laughter. "Voilà," he said, "how can you leave this one behind. Poor Yassi the tailor, with his toothache." He roared again. "No, no, my daughter, he has to come."

Stroganoff looked anxiously at Natasha. "What say you, my darling?"

"Oh, very well," said Natasha. "But," her small mouth set, "not Little Igor."

"And why not Little Igor?" said Aliosha really hurt. "What has poor Little Igor done that he should be left behind?"

"He has dropped me," said Natasha. "In class."

"In class," said Aliosha scornfully. "To complain that you are dropped in class!"

"Percussion," said Nevajno.

"Papoushka," said Natasha seriously, "listen to me. Little

Igor is not the good dancer, his mother was not an English governess, he did not pull Vladimir's hair in the nursery, nor have you chased him off any flower-beds with a stick. He has only just come to Omsk. Why should Little Igor come with us to Petersburg, tell me that? He has not even bought himself an overcoat."

A giant came into the room. He was effulging with astrakhan. Little Igor had not bought an overcoat, but he had got himself a new collar and cuffs.

"It will be cold in Petersburg," he boomed, "but like this, I shall not feel it." He pulled up a chair beside Nevajno.

"You," said Nevajno, "will be St. Peter. You will play it with your eyebrows. For the rest you just stand still." He went back to his brooding.

"What he talk about?" asked Little Igor.

"We do not know," said Stroganoff. He turned anxiously to Natasha.

"Very well," whispered Natasha. "This one can come. But you-know-who, never, never, never!"

"Then it is settled," said Stroganoff pleased, "and I can get to bed early." He looked at the clock.

The door opened. Old Vanka from the bank, half asleep, came trundling in an invalid chair. In it, very much awake, was grandpère Stroganoff. His cheeks were flushed and his eyes were shining.

"Grandpère," said Vladimir. "You, who have not left your apartment for fifteen years, come here to give me your blessing. I am touched." He knelt.

Moysha patted his grandson's head perfunctorily. "Go

with God," he said. He waved him away and addressed the company.

"My children," he said, "I bring you the news that will delight you."

"Aunt Anastasia is dead at last?" asked Aliosha hopefully.

Moysha kept her alive with a shake of his head. "You will not go to Petersburg alone," he proclaimed. "You will not in your youth and inexperience, and," he fixed Aliosha with a bird-like glare, "your stupidity, have to pit yourselves against the sharp wits of the great city. No, my children," he announced, "there will be with you one, older, wiser and much more experienced."

"Nu?" said Stroganoff apprehensively.

"Me," said Moysha, rapping his breast with his bony knuckles. "I will travel there by train," he boasted.

"Aie!" said Aliosha.

Only Natasha retained her presence of mind. She crossed to the old man and kissed him.

"It is noble of you, grandpère," she said, "but we cannot accept this sacrifice. It will be cold in Petersburg," she pointed out, "and the journey will exhaust you. No, mon grandpère," she wheedled, "stay here in little Omsk, in your nice warm apartment, and Vladimir shall write you every day."

"Can't read," said Moysha crossly.

"But, papoushka," said Aliosha.

"Grandpère, listen," said Stroganoff.

"Silence, both of you," said Moysha. "It is decided that I go to Petersburg to see that you do not make fools of yourselves, and also," his face took on the look of a visionary, "to collect the money that many people owe me."

"But, papoushka . . ." said Aliosha.

"Speak when you're spoken to," snapped Moysha. "I have considered this thing in all its bearings and I am decided. I go to Petersburg and Vanka comes with me. Isn't that so, Vanka?"

The old cashier nodded blissfully. "I have always wanted to see the Nevsky Prospekt before I die," he said.

The room at large looked at one another. It shrugged. With fatalistic calm it accepted the position. For was it not Russian? The company embraced the old man. They said how glad they would be to have him with them. They filled hot-water bottles for him, they helped to trundle him into his sleigh, they called "good-bye" as the bells tinkled into the distance and they shouted back at the neighbours. All save Nevajno who sat on brooding into the fire.

"When the Angel of Death it come on, the light it go out," he told the empty room. "It is symbolic," he assured himself.

A quarter to five.

"One last glass of tea," said Stroganoff, "and then ho! for my early night."

"Me, too, I wish for the early night," said Little Igor. He passed up his glass.

"My son," said Aliosha, deeming this the perfect moment, "you will do me the little favour. You know my Katusha?"

Vladimir said he knew Katusha. He said it a shade uneasily.

"Katusha lacks the confidence," said Aliosha. "She does

not like to demand the parts that her talents merit." He paused. "What say you?" he asked.

Natasha said nothing, but she looked a lot.

"So," said Aliosha, "it is the papa who must ask the son for her."

The son shivered. As for Natasha her arms were already akimbo.

"When we get to Petersburg," said Aliosha looking carefully at the ceiling, "you will see to it that it is Katusha who dances the Peri at the first performance."

All was silent save for Little Igor drinking tea.

Natasha, arms still akimbo, looked at Aliosha and defied him.

"It is better that you know at once," she said. "Your Katusha is not coming to Petersburg."

This did not register right away. When it did a dull flush diffused papoushka's face. And then he was on his feet, roaring with rage and knocking down the glass Little Igor was passing up.

"My Katusha!" he said. "My Katusha," he repeated. "MY KATUSHA," he bellowed in capitals. All other words had failed him.

A chair scraped harshly. Nevajno was on his feet.

"It is no use," he said in disgust. "My whole conception it stink."

He strode out. He slammed the front door. He fell down the steps. He shouted back at the neighbours.

"A genius," said Little Igor admiringly.

★　　★　　★

At last the guests had gone. Stroganoff had taken Nevaj-no's chair and was brooding into the fire.

He had lost every battle. Kashkavar Jones was going to St. Petersburg. Little Igor was going, the man who was no Nijinsky was going, that cow Katusha was going. Grand-père was going, Vanka was going, every mediocrity in Omsk was going—except the brothel-keeper. In his hour of bitterness Stroganoff wondered why they had overlooked that one—he'd been in Omsk for years too. What chance would he have to dazzle St. Petersburg with this collection? Might as well stay in Omsk. He kicked moodily at the Louis Quinze.

But this was where Natasha showed her mettle. Young as she was, she realized that, just as there are moments to nag a husband, there are moments not to nag a husband. This was the perfect one.

"Come to bed, my darling," she said. "It will seem much better in the morning." She put an arm on his shoulder. "First things first," she counselled, "and the first thing is that we go to Petersburg. After that we will see."

"Little Igor," said Stroganoff. "The theatre thunders every time he jumps. Kashkavar Jones who cannot point the toe. Katusha!" He kicked the Louis Quinze. "What sort of effect is this we show the Capital?"

Natasha twined the other arm. "Never mind, darling," she said. "I will shine all the more brightly for it."

Stroganoff kissed her arms. He travelled up them, kissing.

"Come to bed," said Natasha.

Stroganoff rose slowly to his feet. He put an arm round

Natasha. "To bed," he agreed. He kissed her warmly. He kissed her more warmly.

But as they drew apart a new blow fell. The clock struck. It was clustered with cupids, but it struck.

"Quelle horreur," said Stroganoff in despair. "My train it go in twenty minutes."

He made for the trunk and jumped on it.

CHAPTER IX

As this was a business trip, Stroganoff took the business-man's train—Russia's latest glory, the Trans-Siberian Express—all the way from St. Petersburg to Vladivostok in under ten days. An average speed of thirty miles an hour! No need to bring your own food, for there was a restaurant car. There was also a captain, just as though the train were a ship, and, if you were a personage, he would invite you to his table. No need to leave the train from start to finish, except, of course, at Irkutsk, where you and your luggage and your literature and your relations got into another train with a new set of as yet untipped attendants, and, of course, a new captain.

And the cost of all this luxury was only double the ordinary fare.

Well worth it, as Stroganoff explained to the comfortably stomached stranger, who had been using the service ever since it started.

"Particularly," he added beaming, "as my papoushka pays."

"So you have the rich father," said the stranger. This plausible, bald-headed young man was by no means the first confidence-trickster he had met on the Trans-Siberian

Express, though it was the first one who had started babbling at him before his luggage was fairly stowed away.

"Voilà," said Stroganoff, unwrapping a travelling rug and furling it round himself. "We are snug here. My little father," he boasted, "is the richest man in Omsk save one—my little grandfather, may he live many years yet."

"He is then the brothel-keeper?" said the stranger, a man of the world.

"Du tout," said Stroganoff coldly. "We are the ballet."

"Ballet," said the stranger, who had a reason of his own (a plump little reason, at the moment poised rather uncertainly in the first row of the corps-de-ballet at Vladivostok) for being interested in the subject. "You have a ballet in Omsk?"

"Omsk," said Stroganoff, "is a very moral town. There, the brothel-keeper is but the fifth richest citizen, and, since my ballet it come, he is, maybe, only the sixth."

Some of the wariness left the stranger. He opened a basket and passed over the leg of a chicken.

"The food in the restaurant is terrible," he explained, "so I bring the little extra."

Stroganoff produced a hip-flask. They feasted together, penduluming the flask and with every nip Stroganoff owned a slice more of the world.

"In what other Opera in all the Russias," he boasted, "will you find a company like ours? Our conductor!" He kissed his fingers. "Our prima ballerina!" He kissed them twice. "I tell you, my friend, she is the little Pavlova, the Trefilova in miniature, the Kshessinskaya of the East. And also," he remembered, "she is my wife."

"Then you married her," said the stranger. He pondered on this. He shook his head. He was married already.

"Voilà!" said Stroganoff. He whipped out a photograph.

"Oho!" said the stranger.

"But," said Stroganoff, "she has a mamoushka."

The stranger passed back the photograph. "Ah," he said sympathetically. There was a mamoushka in Vladivostok, too. He passed over a wing. The flask pendulumed.

"Mamoushka—poof!" said Stroganoff. He flung her off. "Soon we will be in Petersburg," he glanced at the snow-covered landscape crawling past, "and my little pigeon will be the toast of the town."

The landscape stopped. The locomotive was taking in water, or would be directly they had broken the ice.

"Soon," said Stroganoff, "we shall be in the wonderful theatre of our own, where all is telephone and lifts and even the safety curtain," he said in awe, "they tell me will work. And also," he added, "they tell me it will not burn, though of this I am not yet convinced."

The stranger considered. "It is possible," he said. "In Vladivostok we have the curtain that resists the fire—this has been proved. The theatre, you understand, was built of wood, so it perished, but the safety curtain is still there. They are building a new theatre around it. Of wood," he remembered.

"My theatre in Petersburg will be of marble," said Stroganoff, "with gilt on the domes and angels on the ceiling and red plush fauteuils. Almost one could sleep in them." He seized his chin. "Is this good?" he asked, worried.

"It is as well," said the stranger.

"There will be boxes," said Stroganoff. "Many boxes, for all the world of fashion will wish to subscribe and to be seen. The jewels!" He shielded his eyes.

"H'm," said the stranger. The plump little reason had strong views on jewels.

"The dressing-rooms will be warm, the stage vast, all the fountains, the trap-doors, the transformation scenes—we do them like that." Stroganoff flicked his fingers. "And in the orchestra pit there will be ample space so that," a memory came back, "the trombone does not keep hitting the neck of the double bass. And also," he enlarged, "there will be the foyer luxurious with a ceiling of gold and marble pillars and pictures of my ballerinas on the walls, and maybe," he envisaged, "a picture of myself."

"And where," asked the stranger dazzled, "will you find this—this palace?"

"My friend," said Stroganoff, "I have found it already. My little grandfather has given it to me. A great man, my little grandfather," he said. "The trouble I have had to persuade him to come to Petersburg with us! For days I pleaded. And then he say 'Yes,' and I am happy."

The locomotive hooted.

"Your grandfather has many interests in the capital?" asked the stranger.

"Well," said Stroganoff. He considered. "There are many people there that owe much to him."

"Influential," said the stranger. "I see." His voice took on a note of deep respect.

"Big influence," said Stroganoff. "It is this that get me the theatre. The little grandfather he influence the man who own it."

The stranger looked wise.

"Yes," said Stroganoff. "He demand that he pay back the note of his grandfather's hand or else . . ."

The stranger looked a little less wise. But Stroganoff was rambling on.

"So," he said, "we get the theatre suitable. But the owner does not wish to pay his grandfather's note of hand all at once so, for the moment, we get it for three nights a week and every other Sunday."

"I see," said the stranger. He didn't.

"On the other nights," said Stroganoff, "there is some other company, and that one pays with money to the owner. And this," he admitted, "is right, for he must live too."

"And this other company," said the stranger.

"They are the finest in all Russia," said Stroganoff. "No doubt. I do not yet know what they play," he conceded, "but it is probably the Racine and the Oscar Wilde, or something of that nature. You can assure yourself," he said, "that I will look closely into their repertory and I will not tolerate that they play Chekov or any of these modern comedies."

The stranger rummaged in his metropolitan memories. "I laughed at Dead Souls," he said.

"It is most important," said Stroganoff seriously, "that the company who share my theatre shall also share my high artistic standard. For you understand that I shall assemble around me not only the talent of Omsk but the entire intelligentsia of the capital."

"Oho," said the stranger. "Another Diaghilev."

"Diaghilev—poof!" said Stroganoff. "What to me is Diaghilev? Diaghilev," he pointed out pityingly, "has no little grandfather."

CHAPTER X

S<small>T</small>. P<small>ETERSBURG</small> in early spring. General Dumka stopped and bought himself a buttonhole. Who said he was getting old? There was a nip in the air, but it only made his cheeks glow.

The capital, with its domes and spires of snow, was a city in a crystal bowl. Sleighs passed one another, all tinkling bells, cracking whips and puffed-out coachmen. Pedestrians, heavily swathed in furs, waddled along pavements, too wrapped up to bow. The shops were bright avenues of sophisticated Parisian temptation, and here and there a crystal tram clanged angrily at a snow-sweeper to get on with it.

A great city. A proud city. A city to which nothing could ever happen.

General Dumka glowed at it. It was good to be out on this fine spring morning. It was good to be alive. And for the first time since his retirement, it was good to look into the future. For at last he was to take his rightful place in the world of the ballet. No longer would he be just seat number nineteen in the front row of the dress circle—a little too much to the left. When he spoke people would have to listen—even young Diaghilev would have to cock an ear. For was he not about to become the chief patron of a wonderful company from Omsk, and rightly so, for had he not planted the seed that was about to blossom in the great city? Was he not this morning to meet his new bosom-friend, Vladimir Stroganoff, an impresario with vision—even though he might be unsound on Dourakova? And was he not to stay at his elbow at every move, like Nouvel with Diaghilev, counselling and suggesting and attending to every detail? Good as the company from Omsk no doubt was, it would need to recruit fresh glory and he, Dumka, only yesterday cut short by Kshessinskaya's mamoushka, would have the final word in the recruiting. What more could a Russian General require?

General Dumka mounted the marble steps of the Hôtel de l'Europe. It had a revolving door and a commissionaire specially engaged to swivel it. What is more he was already there and swivelling.

General Dumka timed it and passed through. A bald dome pounced on him and swivelled him back into the street again.

"You are retarded, my friend," said Stroganoff. "Hurry or we will be late for class at the Maryinsky."

"The Maryinsky," said Dumka. "We cannot go there. They will not let us in."

"Non?" said Stroganoff surprised. "But I am the impresario from Omsk!"

"Omsk is not enough," said General Dumka sadly.

Stroganoff pondered. "And the little bribe," he said, "does it not then work in the capital?"

St. Petersburg in spring and a lovely morning in Theatre

Street. Snow brightened the ledges and crowned the façades of the classical avenue which ended in the State Theatre and flanked and contained all that stood for theatrical tradition in Imperial Russia. Here, cut off from the vulgarity of the city, in rooms of classical proportions, stood the schools, the dormitories, the rehearsal rooms, the wardrobes and the students' theatre.

Here sloe-eyed children of ten came every year to show their paces to an assembly of implacable judges. The more fortunate children were swallowed whole into the mystery; to be fed, clothed and scolded more thoroughly than they would have been at home, to be submitted to a rigorous discipline of muscle, mind and behaviour, and to emerge seven years later, not as full-fledged ballerinas—oh no! but just about fit to be risked in a pas de six on some not too important occasion, and so privileged to carry, in their turn, the flaming torch of the Maryinsky tradition. And such was the strength of the training that, in spite of its weight, few found the torch too heavy, though lately there had been a distressing tendency to abandon it for marriage or for Diaghilev. Teleyakov, the State Director, disapproved strongly of both. The first was inevitable more or less, but for the second there could be no excuse. These dancers owed a duty to the State, which had fed, clothed, perfected and helped to keep them safe from the snares of the world and dependent great-aunts. . . .

"The Maryinsky," explained Stroganoff to the sandy man, "might request a dancer to leave, but for a dancer to request to leave the Maryinsky . . ." He threw up his arms. "No," he said, "my good friend Teleyakov did not like my good friend Diaghilev."

"Who didn't like what?" asked the sandy man. He blinked.

"Alors," said Stroganoff, "we are in St. Petersburg in the early spring . . ."

A fine morning in Theatre Street.

The sentry on guard outside the seminary was stamping the blood back into his toes. He wished he were a dancer and could keep his feet warm. But papoushka had been against it. This had been the blow that broke mamoushka's heart, and not the Other Woman, as his grand-mamoushka had always insisted. How had he got into the guards? He couldn't remember.

Teleyakov passed through the portals. The sentry clicked his heels and saluted. Diaghilev came through. The sentry saluted. With light steps the ballerinas came hurrying in. The sentry winked at them. Wiry little girls with their hair brushed back, and tough little boys, with their hair un-brushed, raced one another to the doors. The sentry cuffed them. One of the cooks came staggering through laden with two baskets. The sentry gave him a hand. "To-morrow," he said, "we will both be rich." To-morrow was the day of the State Lottery.

General Dumka turned into the avenue. With him was a pair of yellow boots from the provinces. They squeaked. The sentry stopped them.

"Gentlemen," he said, "your carte d'entrée."

They passed it. It was a ten-rouble note.

"Quite in order," said the sentry. "But remember," he warned them, "I have not seen you."

A lovely morning in Theatre Street. The sun came slanting in through the great windows of the practice-room in the State Theatre. It gilded the bare calm wall, it glanced across the barre that had sustained so many sweating featherweights, it reflected from the shiny grand piano (perfectly tuned), and on to the pianist, who was not a beaky old lady with chilblains and a cold. It shone back, a thousand discs of radiance, from the chandeliers and it touched the room warmly to life so that the people moving in the great mirrors seemed as real as the people moving in the great room. It reflected the dancers in practice costumes waiting for the maestro to arrive and limbering up as they waited—and never an odd ballet shoe among them. It reflected a group of intelligent ravens on small gilt chairs lining a corner of the classroom, attendant on a larger raven, with a single white lock, perched on an equally hard chair.

Sergei Diaghilev, at the moment not yet edged out of his position as artistic adviser to the Maryinsky, had the right to attend all classes, and, though he generally failed to get up in time, this morning he had done it. He had reasons of his own, which Teleyakov, the State Director, would certainly not have approved, for wishing to study this class.

Stroganoff and General Dumka, admitted unobtrusively to a well-bribed recess and told to remain unobserved and act as though they belonged there, had much the same reason for attending class as Diaghilev, though rather worse prospects.

"The maestro," said Stroganoff despondently, "I have to bribe him too?"

"Sssh," said General Dumka horrified.

In the centre of the room a young man was leaping and beating the air.

"Come down, Vatza," called the ballerina Karsavina. "Let us try the lifts in Lac."

But Nijinsky went on jumping as though he had not heard. He was clumsy this morning. He must limber up before the maestro came. Only entre chat-huit so far. Pfui!

The other dancers, too, were working, each after her own fashion. It was as well to be supple before the maestro arrived, for who knew what mood he might arrive in? They went on working like devils possessed.

The door opened. Not a heart but missed a beat. Not a hand but made to cross itself.

The maestro was coming in.

"Non, non, non, non! Aie, aie, aie! You dance like poodles —all of you! And you!" The stick came down on a thigh with a thwack.

It was all right. The maestro was in a good mood on this bright spring day.

The piano tinkled. The stick banged. The maestro moved among his sweating pupils, encouraging them after his own manner.

"And you, Mathilde. What is this effect that you give us?"

What time were you back from the Cubat last night? No, do not tell me, for you will only lie."

The divine Kshessinskaya, Ballerina Assoluta of the Maryinsky Theatre, the darling of the metropolis, who was to marry a grand duke and who lived in a little palace of her own, the naughty little Mathilde went scarlet.

"But I drink the nothing," she excused herself. "One little glass of Mumm, and that only because of Svetlov entreated me."

The maestro produced a handkerchief. He dried her eyes. He patted her cheek. "Don't do it again, little poodle," he said. He turned on another straining back. "The heel," he rapped, "raised. The 'ip in. The back strong." He stood back and regarded the perfect line. "Ah," he said, "that is better. It begins now to resemble an arabesque."

"But it is not bad—the arabesque," said Stroganoff to General Dumka. He tilted his head. "Ma foi, it is not bad at all."

"It is Karsavina," said Dumka in tones of mingled reproof and prayer.

Anyone else would have hung his head. But not Vladimir.

"And they treat her like this," he said indignantly. "I make her the offer for my company. How much, you think, will she ask?"

"You are too late, my friend," said Dumka. "It is rumoured that she goes again with Diaghilev to Europe."

"Is it signed?" asked Stroganoff keenly.

Diaghilev, too, had been watching the arabesque.

"Exasperating," he said.

"Taya is being difficult again?" asked Nouvel, sitting next to him.

"If it were only that," said Diaghilev. He sighed. "First she will come to us and then she won't. Then she must dance all the rôles and then not any of them, then it is more money and then it is the guarantee that I will pay it. I tell you that if I did not need her so much I would tell her to go to," he pondered, "Omsk," he substituted.

Nouvel looked at Stroganoff. "Your rival?" He grinned.

Diaghilev did not smile. "Do not underrate the provincial," he said. "If he can get his hand on money he can be a nuisance."

Nouvel eyed Stroganoff again. He noted the bright yellow boots.

"What nonsense, Sergei," he said. "Which ballerina would go to him when she could come to us?"

"You can never tell what a ballerina will decide to do," said Diaghilev gravely. "Particularly," he added just as gravely, "when she is in a temper."

A small bundle of femininity came into the room, hurried to the barre, lifted a leg, and tried to look as though she had been there all the time. This ballerina was late. So it was the maestro who decided to be in a temper.

"Arenskaya," breathed Dumka devoutly through the falling heavens.

"So, my darling," said the maestro, an adder about to strike, "you have slept deeply—yes?"

Arenskaya clutched the barre. She had to face the cataclysm, she had to survive it, and what is more, she had to survive it without bursting into tears. She threw out her chin.

"The chin—in," said the maestro. He slapped it.

"Did they forget your morning tea, my darling?" he pursued, "or was it that your dear friend was loath to leave you?" He looked at her. "No," he said, "it could not have been that."

Arenskaya breathed in. She clenched her teeth. She shot a look at the maestro containing everything she must not say. But the maestro had turned away. An expert, he knew he could not improve on his last remark.

"Alors," he rapped. "Centre practice, my little darlings."

Wistfully the perfection class of the Maryinsky Theatre abstracted itself from Arenskaya's dilemma and took up positions that were certain to lead to dilemmas of their own.

"Ah—that class of perfection." To the sandy man's horror there were tears in Stroganoff's eyes. "Trefilova, Egorova, Preobrajenskaya, Karsavina, Kyasht, Nijinsky," the names were all part of his personal litany. "And Pavlova," he crowned them, "though, also, she was not at class that day. All young, all ravishing, all with their future before them, all working—all working hard—in that room. And I," he shook his head, "I was young, too, and perhaps a little silly, though you might not guess it. What are they now?" he looked into the present. "They are old ladies and they teach in Paris and they hope to find a talent as great as theirs. And me, the old man with the stomach, I know that it does not exist."

"What about Robert Helpmann?" asked the sandy man.

But Stroganoff had not heard. "Ah, those were the days. All those Goddesses," he mourned, "in one room, and I," he sighed, nostalgia getting the better of truth, "privileged to go and watch them at their practice whenever I wished. To think," he said sorrowfully, "that there were mornings when I did not do it." He paused to regret it. "And to-day," he said, "you have to cross the Atlantic to see Anton Dolin."

The piano tinkled. The stick banged. The maestro sat and gazed non-committally at his pupils.

Egorova, Trefilova, Preobrajenskaya, Karsavina, Kyasht, Kshessinskaya, and the Little Lopokova.

No Pavlova, the maestro noted. Resting! Never heard of such a thing!

"Alors," he said. He waved his hands.

The class stood aside while Egorova, Trefilova and Kshessinskaya watched the old man as he devised a complicated enchaînement with his fingers. They sailed through it.

"Disgraceful," said the maestro. "Bad, bad, bad. You dance like a circus."

Egorova, Trefilova and Kshessinskaya went through it again.

"Mon Dieu," said Stroganoff. "And I thought that the class at Omsk was good!" He wept.

Karsavina, Lopokova and Kyasht took the floor, floated flawlessly, and were duly chided by the maestro. They floated again.

"My friend," said Stroganoff. "What am I dreaming of? What use to bring my ballet to St. Petersburg." He got up.

"I go back to Omsk," he announced.

The paling Dumka tugged him back. "Courage, Vladimir," he said. "Your troubles but begin."

On the floor someone else's troubles had begun. Arenskaya had overbalanced.

It was too much for the maestro. His gentle irony left him. It left him spitting, clawing and screaming. Terrified, Arenskaya backed. The maestro, bent almost double in a combination of fury and old age, hobbled after her, screaming as he hobbled. Backing and screaming they arrived at the corner of the room where Stroganoff and Dumka were trying to look as though they were not there.

They need not have troubled.

"You," screamed the maestro, "you will get out of my class. You will never come back. You will never let me see your silly face again, nor your deformed développé, nor your bent arabesque, nor," he paused to find the final insult, "nor your big behind."

"It is not big," screamed Arenskaya suddenly. A ballerina can stand just so much. "I take myself from your class. I take me from your stupid teaching. I take me from the whole Maryinsky. I take me from the world." She wept.

"Out!" quivered the maestro. "Out—before my heart it attack me."

"Out," advised the class in an urgent whisper. "Go now and apologize later."

"Apologize, never!" Arenskaya defied them. "You shall all crawl to me. All. You shall eat your word when I get me the other contract. The contract stupendous." She looked straight at Diaghilev.

But Diaghilev, a diplomat if ever there was one, was deep in conversation with Benois.°

"I go," said Arenskaya despairingly. "I go—not to come back no more."

She waited. Nobody said don't. Blind with rage she made for the door.

A bald dome leapt after her, unfolding a document as he leapt.

"Sign," panted Stroganoff. "Sign quick."

Blind with rage, Arenskaya seized the fountain pen and scribbled. "Voilà!" she said. A thought struck her. "Mon Dieu, what is it that I have signed?" She tried to snatch it back.

But Stroganoff held the document safely behind him.

"It is the contract stupendous," he told her reassuringly.

The maestro marvelled at himself. Why wasn't he having a heart attack?

"Out, out, out, out, out!" he screamed.

He was.

° Footnote to faithful readers: 'E 'ad come—clearly 'e was not yet 'imself.

CHAPTER XI

L<small>UNCH.</small>

A quiet little restaurant round the corner.

Everybody went there.

It was the perfect place for confidential conversations. Though everybody could be heard by everybody else, you could be quite confident that not one of them would be listening.

Dancers have themselves to talk about.

"My flowers . . ." said Karsavina, from a table in the corner.

"My public . . ." said Kshessinskaya from a centre table.

"My mamoushka," said Trefilova, Egorova and Preobrajenskaya. But they were saying it at different tables.

"Where can I get some ballet shoes?" mused Nijinsky, who wore his out more quickly than the State could supply them.

"My career," said Arenskaya fiercely. "You wish that I bury my whole career in Omsk!"

"Not Omsk, my darling," soothed Dumka for the seventh time. "This is only the town which our dear friend here has left for ever."

The three of them were seated at the draughtiest table in

the room. They had come here to cement the contract with the friendly little luncheon. They had ordered champagne, but it had not yet arrived, and the little repast delicious, which would, no doubt, be served in due course. And in the meantime Stroganoff and Dumka were impressing their first ballerina with the opportunities for glory hovering over the contract she had so rashly signed, just before they were thrown out of the Maryinsky.

Arenskaya needed a lot of convincing.

"Me," she said, "the most admired 'ips of all, and you bury them in Omsk."

"Ah—the champagne," said Stroganoff thankfully. It was a little warm, but he poured it out. And as Arenskaya stopped weeping to drink, he seized his chance.

"Not Omsk," he said. "The theatre magnificent in Petersburg—with the name in my valise."

"And you," said Dumka, "shall be the leading ballerina."

"Save, of course," said Stroganoff, "for my wife."

A loyal remark, but tactless.

"In your company," declared Arenskaya, a crouching cat, "I dance as Assoluta or not at all. Is this not in my contract?"

"It is not," said Stroganoff, apprehensively.

At his corner table, Diaghilev began to enjoy himself, though you would never have thought it to look at him. The Provincial was learning. Soon he would begin to understand that it was not so easy to run a ballet company.

"I must go to little Ginsberg again," he told Fokine. "He must get me more money somehow."

The waiter trundled a trolley of zakuski across the floor. Caviar, smoked salmon, foie gras, prawns in aspic—delicious! He pulled up at the table on the far side of Arenskaya and kept an anxious eye on the dishes as he served.

"It will turn to ashes in my mouth," declared Arenskaya, helping herself lavishly.

"And that, my friend," Stroganoff told the sandy man, "was the beginning of the comradeship that has lasted all my life. We have worked together, we have starved together, we have laughed together, and we have wept together. Always, always Arenskaya has been at my side—except for when she walk out on me—advising, helping and encouraging. If she were my darling daughter," he said, "she could not love me more."

The door opened. The loving daughter, an aged crow in a nasty temper, hurried in.

"I spit me of your company," she shrilled. "I leave tomorrow, no—sooner. I go at once." She stayed where she was. "You are the dishonest rogue, the crooked one, the thief of Baghdad." Uplifted by her own rhetoric she turned on the sandy man.

"I do not exaggerate," she assured him. "He is the Prince of Ali Babas and prison is too good for him."

"'Ush," said Stroganoff. "Less loud. The rich one he comes at any moment." He looked anxiously at the door.

"Bon," said Arenskaya. "I wait for him." She sat down. She glared at Pavlova. "I tell him all—all," she assured the photograph. She fixed Stroganoff with a quivering claw. "I tell him how you stew the books and make the fool of the income tax collector, the poor trusting one, and rob the noble England that has given you so much and also the visa."

" 'Ush," said Stroganoff more loudly. "Shoot oop, or I talk back. I tell the rich one how in your trunk there are two bottles of brandy of which you tell the poor deluded customs nothing. Not one word," he assured the sandy man. "She ogle and she show him the little packet of cigarettes."

"It is you who drink the brandy," screamed Arenskaya. "And also," she remembered, a broken woman, "smoke the cigarettes! Wait," she encouraged herself. "Wait till the rich one comes. Wait till I tell him how you rob everyone, and how," she waved a slit-open pay envelope, "you have just rob me."

"Poof," said Stroganoff uneasily, "it will not be of interest."

"He will put you in prison," said Arenskaya with relish, "and you will eat your English skilly, and me, I shall sit outside the cell and drink the champagne."

The sandy man, an unfledged dove, tried to reconcile the two old friends.

"Poor Mr. Stroganoff," he said. "What has he done? Perhaps he didn't mean it . . ." Before the two-pronged glare that was switched on him by both assailants, he tailed off.

"Done," screamed Arenskaya. "I will tell you what he has done, and you will see for yourself that never has there been such a monster." She took a deep breath. "When we get to London, I need the new dress for the opening night, *his* opening night," she pointed out. "Is it not natural that I wish to do him credit? And he say to me, this monster of perfidity, he say, 'Go and get it, my darling.' And I think he is generous, and I kiss him and go. And now, figurez-vous," she flung out an arm, "he begin to deduct it from my salary. Me—an old woman!"

"And did I tell you, an old woman," thundered Stroganoff, "to spend yourself the fifty pounds so that you look like a schoolgirl who has grown too quick."

Arenskaya's heel tapped. "Now," she said, "now—he insult me." She turned on the sandy man. "Why you not knock him down?"

"I defend myself," said Stroganoff. He sprang up and crouched behind his fists.

"Why not split the difference," said the sandy man swiftly.

Arenskaya looked at him with cold contempt. "So you are both against me," she declared. "Very well—I invoke the British justice. We have the court case and the judge make me the compliments on my hat—all feathers. I go to my solicitor to arrange this now."

Full of dignity she made for the door. On the threshold she turned. "If the mirror in the classroom is not mend by to-morrow, I," she paused for the awful threat, "will not take the class."

She swept out.

"It is the third time that the slipper it slip from her hand," confided the suddenly subsided Stroganoff. He shrugged. "What signifies a broken mirror so long as she is happy while she breaks it! Ah, my friend," he said, "the ballet it might go on without Arenskaya, but then it would go on without me." He looked fondly at the photograph on his desk. "I will pay the fifty pounds," he said, "but only after the hard struggle, or else, you understand, she will buy the new dress every day."

"Then this little—er—contretemps," said the sandy man, "was not entirely unexpected?"

Stroganoff beamed. "My friend," he said, "I have been awaiting it all morning."

The friendly little lunch was growing friendlier. The champagne might be warm, but so was the food. Under the influence of both, Arenskaya had settled down to make the best of what she had signed, and so, save by wheedling, could not help.

Flushed by his success, Stroganoff had grown more and more ambitious. Not a dancer at the Maryinsky but was visualized, signed up, rehearsed and making the appearance triumphant at the theatre with the name in the valise. He waved away the two obstacles that sprang up monotonously as each name danced across the table—first Arenskaya's dead body, over which it appeared each dancer would have to be dragged, and next Dumka's forebodings that they were signed by Diaghilev already. He gulped more champagne, scribbled down telephone numbers, and urged Dumka to contact them without further waste of time.

"Have in me the confidence," he urged. "I know I come only from Omsk, but," he glowed, "I have the vision."

"You visualize me as the Assoluta," said Arenskaya back to her battements.

"Si, si," said General Dumka. He patted her shoulder.

"Alors," said Stroganoff, "to work, mes amis. You," he told Dumka, "shall speak of our project to the ballerinas. You, my star," he looked thoughtfully at Arenskaya, "shall go and rest yourself after the emotions of the morning. I send you some roses." He made a note. "And I," he gloated, "shall go and look at my beautiful theatre. But first," he remembered, "I must go to my valise."

General Dumka raised his glass. "To our beautiful theatre," he toasted.

Stroganoff raised his. "To our beautiful ballerina," he said.

Arenskaya raised hers. "To our season." She drank. She caught sight of Karsavina and Kyasht, two interested angels at the centre table. They should crawl! Crawl! "To our glorious season," she amended. She drank again.

CHAPTER XII

E ARLY morning in St. Petersburg. The spires and domes of the holy city lay peacefully beneath their eiderdowns of snow waiting for the sun to touch them to life. Even the great railway station looked like the snow queen's palace—from the outside. Inside all was draught and depression.

The booking clerk was wondering why anybody should want to go anywhere and took it as a personal affront that they should disturb him to do it. The porters swore and blew on their fingers and sighed for the revolution—meantime they were determined not to be found anywhere.

But the most depressed figure of all was that of Vladimir Stroganoff, pacing up and down what he hoped was the right platform. Yet this was the hour when his company was to arrive from Omsk, the end of the overture and the curtain going up.

Stroganoff sighed. Two weeks in the capital had wrought a deep change in our optimistic impresario. It had been a terrible two weeks. Getting the company together had proved a nightmare instead of a series of triumphant toasts. Old Dumka had rushed around, promising and pleading, but either the ballerina approached had already signed with

101

Diaghilev or she said "Omsk" and changed the conversation. Men were easier to find, indeed, a number had been engaged, but they were no Nijinskys, and, as Stroganoff fiercely pointed out, he had one of these already.

One coup they had achieved—Ivan Ivanoff by name, Nevajno's bosom friend, who spat every time the choreographer's name was mentioned. But no doubt this was merely his eccentric way of expressing appreciation.

But for the rest, whether it was dancers or painters or composers or dressmakers, or anything at all of the first excellence, there was always an obstacle and always it turned out to be the same obstacle—Sergei Diaghilev. Either Diaghilev had got in first, which was hopeless, or the party was still waiting to be approached by him, which at the best meant delay, indecision and a long haggle.

For ever since Diaghilev had come back from Paris, where the triumph of his Russian opera and ballet had started a fashion, all St. Petersburg had been dazzled—save the bankers. Last year Diaghilev had conquered Paris, this year it was to be Europe. And everybody wanted to be in on it—save the bankers.

Paris, thought Stroganoff. Poof! What was Paris? What did they know of ballet there? Europe! What was a European tour? What wouldn't he give to have one of his own? Instead of the theatre of his little grandfather!

The theatre magnificent! Ha!

Stroganoff tried to think of something else. Soon he would see his Natasha. He would clasp her in his arms. She would ask him many questions. He grew depressed again.

A certain excitement became noticeable on the platform.

Porters, like reluctant rabbits, came out of their burrows and a very old man trundled a samovar on to the platform and fortified himself from it while he waited for the rush.

With a triumphant hoot the engine pulled up. Natasha's little head was bobbing out of a carriage window.

Stroganoff's troubles dropped from him and he sprinted towards it.

"My darling, it is a hundred years," Stroganoff embraced his bride.

"Vladimir, Vladimir," said the smothered Natasha.

"Mind her hat," said mamoushka.

"So this is St. Petersburg," said Kashkavar Jones. He looked round. "Not so big as London," he hazarded a guess.

"My fur collar," mourned Little Igor. "Moth," he pointed.

"Alors, alors, to eat," said papoushka. He linked himself on to Katusha, who was standing in that part of the queue that had not yet kissed Vladimir.

"My native city!" observed Nevajno, "Pfui!"

A warming reunion. But in one more sentence it was over.

"And now," said Natasha on tiptoe with excitement, "take me to see my theatre."

A finger of frost touched Stroganoff's spine. "Presently, my darling," he said. "Presently. But first," he said, "we have the breakfast delicious at the boarding-house." He looked depressed.

"I am too excited to eat," said Natasha. "Let us go now— now!"

"You are tired, my darling," said Stroganoff. "You have

been many days on the train. You want the little bath refreshing." He thought of the worn-off enamel. "The little slumber to restore you," he thought of the rattling shutter and the rock-like mattress, "and then," he finished manfully, "I take you to the theatre."

"Come," said papoushka, "let us eat."

"No," said Natasha firmly. "I must go to my theatre at once." She stamped her foot. "At once, Vladimir."

"At once, Vladimir," said mamoushka. She started.

"We come, too," said the rest of the company. They tugged at their baggage.

"Me," said the papoushka obstinately, "I go and eat." He stamped off.

Nevajno stamped after him. Somebody might as well pay for his breakfast.

Early as it was, there was a line of droshkies outside the station. The company collared the lot, loaded on their luggage, piled themselves inside, and, a stream of triumph, jingled their way into the heart of the city.

"We must be nearly there," said the man who was no Nijinsky expectantly.

They jingled out again.

"It is very far, this theatre," said mamoushka, suspiciously.

"It is a very slow driver," said Stroganoff quickly. They jingled on.

"Look," said Little Igor, pointing to a poster showing a trainer about to pounce on a lion. "A circus! I must go."

"It will not be as good as the one that came to Omsk," said Katusha loyally.

"In Londres," said Kashkavar Jones, "there is a bigger circus—the biggest circus in the world where everybody goes. It is called," he said, "Pic-a-dolly, I think. Often my mamoushka go there." He sighed.

They jingled on.

"It is very far, this theatre," said Natasha. Her mamoushka nodded grimly.

"It depends from where you start," said Stroganoff firmly.

And they jingled on some more and eventually they reached the Theatre Boris Goudonov and the company stood and admired while Stroganoff paid off the droshkies.

The Theatre Boris Goudonov had been triumphantly constructed many years ago. It combined, in a burst of generosity, the worst features of many types of architecture. This was because so many architects had resigned in rage during its construction and each succeeding architect had had firm ideas of his own, while the owner had been equally firm in refusing to scrap anything already built. But the cluster of golden mushrooms that formed the roof had glistened when the paint was new, and everybody's grandparents on the opening night had marvelled as expected at the enormous shining chandeliers, the drinking fountain in the vestibule and the crimson plush of the fauteuils. How pleased the Official Receiver had been!

But that was nearly a hundred years ago. Now the gold had turned green, the paint was peeling, and St. Petersburg had meanly chosen other spots as its fashionable quarters.

But the company from Omsk was eager to be impressed. All save the mamoushka.

"Ah," they said. They stood back and looked at their theatre. "Ah," they said again.

"It is very large," said Little Igor loyally.

"But, my friend," Stroganoff shook a remembering head, "it was no use. Already I knew that the goose could not be kept in the bag and that soon my company must know that the debt to my little grandfather had been paid with the pup in the poke. The Theatre Boris Goudonov was . . ." he felt for the word.

"Not good enough," said the sandy man archly.

Stroganoff looked at him gravely. "You are right, my friend," he said. "It was not good enough."

"Shabby old barn! What man of fashion," demanded the mamoushka angrily, "would come to such a circus!"

"Voilà," said Stroganoff quickly.

A fashionable figure was making its way down the unswept stairs. Long-stemmed roses burgeoned from its arms and a ribbon flew out in the wake of its progress.

It was General Dumka.

"Mille pardons," he bowed low to Natasha. "Nothing but business of the most urgent would have kept me from welcoming you at the station." He presented the flowers and while Natasha raved over them and the mamoushka counted the blooms and the other mamoushkas looked enviously on and saw that she didn't cheat, he drew Stroganoff to one side.

"Novikoff," he hissed, "says No."

"He goes to Diaghilev?" hissed Stroganoff.

"It is not yet settled," peeved Dumka. "It is agreed only that he does not come to us."

"Voilà!" said Stroganoff hopefully. "The auditorium."

The company gasped. All those seats to be filled! All that plush!

"The company that play the Racine and the Oscar Wilde," said Little Igor doubtfully, "they draw the town?"

"My friend," said General Dumka, "they pack the house."

The company closed its eyes. For a moment it could not see the red plush for bare shoulders shining with diamonds. For a moment the golden dome was ringing with bravas! The man who was no Nijinsky gave a little skip.

"Vladimir," said the mamoushka, peering keenly along the edge of the stage. "What is this that looks like sawdust?"

"Sawdust," said Stroganoff firmly.

They went backstage.

"Voilà, my darling," said Stroganoff, arriving outside a vermilion door. "Your dressing-room. The star's dressing-room," he added, and flung it open.

Inside was Arenskaya. She was well installed. She must have brought all her possessions, including a baby sea lion that howled immediately.

"Pardon," said Stroganoff. He made to close the door.

But Arenskaya was on her feet and cooing over Natasha. So does a serpent coo at a rabbit.

"Ah," she said, "the little one from Omsk. But your travelling hat is charming—charming. I had one just like this last year! I am sorry now that I have given it to the maid—she does not know how to wear it, that one."

Natasha looked round for her mamoushka. But the mamoushka was in the corridor frowning at what looked exactly like an elephant.

"Pardon," said Stroganoff quickly, "I make the introduce. My little wife," he kissed the no-time-to-snatch-away hand. "Our new friend, Arenskaya, who has come to the company."

"As Assoluta," said Arenskaya sweetly. "We will be the great friends," she followed up her advantage, "see if we are not. Watch me closely and you will learn much, my dear. They tell me," she said kindly, "that already you show much promise."

Once again Natasha looked round for her mamoushka. But mamoushka was still gazing at what still seemed to be an elephant. So Natasha joined battle alone.

"You are very kind," she said, "and I am very cross with Vladimir that he did not tell you this was the dressing-room of the star. Now," she was all sympathy, "you have all the trouble of moving."

But before Arenskaya could reply Stroganoff had intervened.

"Mais non," he said, "it is I who make the mistake. I explain outside," he hissed to Natasha. "Come."

"Vladi-mir!" The voice of the mamoushka floated sharply into the room. Once and for all she meant to decide was this, or was this not an elephant?

"Quick," said Stroganoff. He raced his little bride in the opposite direction and they had mounted a flight of stairs before she had found her breath.

"I take you to your dressing-room," panted Stroganoff.

"It is the real star's dressing-room," he assured her, "but do not tell Arenskaya this."

"Above stage level? So?" said Natasha. Her little mouth set.

Stroganoff flew her along a corridor flanked with tanks with fishes in them. At the other end of it was the coming-up mamoushka.

"Vladimir," she pointed to a tank. "Tell me the truth. Is that, or is that not, an octopus?" In a dazed fashion she counted.

"Presently," said Vladimir, and flew his bride down another flight of stairs. He avoided the elephant and flung open a Prussian blue door.

"Voilà," he said, "the star's dressing-room."

In it was a lion. It was in a wheelable cage and it was asleep, but it was a lion.

Stroganoff gave up the struggle. He stood silent as the rest of the company crowded in and looked at the lion and looked at each other and looked at their mamoushkas and wondered what to say.

"This . . . other company," said Natasha at last. "This company that plays the Racine and the Oscar Wilde, is it by chance," the syllables fell like ice, "a circus?"

The company held its breath.

Stroganoff turned away.

"Oui," he said heavily.

CHAPTER XIII

Tʜᴇ great day had come. It was snowing.

To-night the Ballet Stroganoff from Omsk opened in St. Petersburg.

To-night the Theatre Boris Goudonov would be packed with a critical, appraising, cosmopolitan audience—balletomanes to a brassière.

To-night General Dumka would wear all his medals. To-night Stroganoff would make a speech.

To-night ballerinas would be wildly elated or beating their bosoms. To-night their mamoushkas would be elated with them or beat their bosoms even harder.

To-night was to be a triumph.

To-night Stroganova would take her six curtains.

But at the moment it was the répétition generale. Not, by common consent, sufficiently general to let in the critics, but, by common resignation, insufficiently private to keep out the circus.

Even what had turned out to be definitely an elephant was looking on from the vast recesses of the wings. Whatever this was, it was certainly no circus.

In fact, it was the ballet Sylvia, which had drawn all

110

Paris—for forty years—and which Stroganoff, in a cauldron of seething mamoushkas, had selected for his opening night. For, as sitting alone in the stalls he explained to his stomach-patting papoushka, it contained Sylvia, the part delicious and not too difficult for Natasha, and Cupid, which with a little rearrangement and a seasoning of solos, had been made large enough to satisfy Arenskaya—except, of course, in the billing.

"And my Katusha?" asked Aliosha suspiciously.

"She is the Goddess Diane," said Stroganoff.

Papoushka considered. "Has she got a pas seul?" he asked.

"She dominate the stage," said Stroganoff.

"Ah," said papoushka. "But has she got a pas seul?"

"She is in her temple," said Stroganoff, "and all kneel to her."

"But has she got a pas seul?" said papoushka. Almost he might have been a mamoushka.

"You will see," said Stroganoff tactfully. He changed the subject. "We were right," he said, gazing at the fauns and dryads limbering up on the stage, "to choose a ballet Petersburg has not seen for many years. The music is familiar, the story is old, but it is easy to follow and it calls for no one to compare with Nijinsky. Further," he finished in triumph, "no one can say they do it better at the Maryinsky for," he pointed out, "they do not do it at all."

A depressed General Dumka wandered in and flopped into the stall beside Stroganoff.

"Kyasht," he said despairingly, "refuses."

"Why you tell me this now," said Stroganoff annoyed.

"Have I not enough to despair myself with already?"

And he looked at the side of the stage where a piece of canvas had been spread flat and was being painted in a great hurry by a man who, finished or not, had to leave it that afternoon to add a dado to Carnaval, for Diaghilev.

For St. Petersburg was not Omsk. In Omsk, Stroganoff of the Opera had but to beckon, whether for a dresser or a droshki, to be overwhelmed by a rush of applicants, all eager, all voluble, all proud to be in his employ, all asking to be remembered to the grand-papoushka. But in St. Petersburg, Stroganoff of the Opera was only the man from Omsk, and if anyone listened to him it was a great favour and if they worked for him it was a great expense. He boasted, he begged, he bribed, he beguiled, he sent bouquets and bought bottles of champagne, but always he was confronted by the brick wall of the Maryinsky, and, if he scaled that, it was only to meet Diaghilev on the other side. Soon it began to look as though the man who was no Nijinsky would have to be leading dancer after all. Presently it was a certainty.

"Good God," said the sandy man.

"But it was not so terrible—this," said Stroganoff. "You must understand, my friend, that there was then only one Nijinsky. He stood alone. There were many dancers who," he waved an arm, "did not drop the ballerina, but only one Nijinsky. So whether it is a trusted friend from Omsk, who dance bad, or some grasping newcomer who dance only a little better, who is to support my Natasha—it make small difference. I am clear—yes?"

"Completely," said the sandy man. "I can almost follow you."

"You must understand, my friend," said Stroganoff, "that the technique of the dancers then is not as we know it now. Then all was tradition, the school, the line, the conductor who watch the stage. Then the ballerina took her preparation and went into her two turns and the house applauded. And if she do thirty-two fouettés the house go mad, all save a few die-difficults, who purse their lips and say it is clever but it is the circus. And these ballerinas," said Stroganoff marvelling, "all school, all line, all authority, they have produce the generation of little spinning tops that you see all over the world to-day. Baronova, Toumanova, Riaboushinska, even the little Fonteyn," he laughed indulgently, "they spin." He waggled his wrist.

"And Natasha?" asked the sandy man.

"She did not spin," said Stroganoff gravely. "She was a flower in porcelain, a china butterfly, when she come on," he raised his arms, "the stage light up, whether it is Omsk, Petersburg, Paris, or any city in the world. C'est une petite ange, my Natasha. She has a charm that none can resist, least of all," he gazed into the past, "me."

The door opened. The present came in. A woman in black, a cottage loaf in a good humour, waddled across the room and kissed Stroganoff. Stroganoff pinched her cheek.

"So you are happy at last, my pigeon," he asked. "Your little daughter has the six curtains and from now on we have only the good fortune—no?"

The cottage loaf stiffened slightly. "The six curtains and the empty house," she said. "You have kept your word, Vladimir, but do not think that this is enough. To-night we have the six curtains again—and to the house full."

The sandy man looked at the cottage loaf. He took in the bulging legs balanced on high heels, the over-tight black satined behind, the three rows of pearls on the bulging bosom, the hat with the black ostrich feathers, the white face, the eyelashes stiff with mascara. He decided he could resist her quite easily.

But Stroganoff was patting her hand.

"Not to-night," he was saying, "the little one does not dance to-night."

"To-night," said the cottage loaf, "dances the one that stamp out from the Inglesby."

"That is so," said Stroganoff unmoved. "But remember, she stamp out."

"Me, I do not stamp out," declared the cottage loaf. "I stay till you arrange the six curtains for my little one."

Stroganoff considered. "Maybe," he suggested, "on the first night of the new Nevajno."

"That old 'am," said the cottage loaf. This was blasphemy, but fortunately God was not there to hear. "You wish that our curtains be mixed with cat-calls?"

"If there are cat-calls," said Stroganoff, by no means rejecting the possibility, "you are sure at least that the audience is still there." He turned to the sandy man for approval. Certainly he was getting none from the cottage loaf. The fingers were tapping, and so was the toe.

"We do the Sugar Plum here in London, us," she demanded. "Do not forget we do the Sugar Plum."

"I will remember," said Stroganoff. "Rest assured that I will remember . . ."

"You will," said the cottage loaf. "Rest assured that you will—for I will continue to remind you."

She rose. Stroganoff kissed her hand.

"Go to your hotel, my pigeon," he said. "You will find there the little surprise from Bond Street."

"The ruby clip I see in the window!" The cottage loaf was gratified but also surprised. "Vladimir—how you afford this thing for me?"

"I talk a little and they give me the credit," said Stroganoff comfortably. "I tell them that the rich one come soon to pay for my extravagances."

"Vladimir—you are a darling," cried the cottage loaf. Her beam embraced the pensive-looking sandy man. "Always he spoil me." She waddled to the door. "If the rich one make the hully-brou-ha-ha," she announced, "I give it back." She considered. "But only then," she decided. She walked out.

"So that was Natasha," said the sandy man.

"All gold, my Natasha," said Stroganoff fondly. "And still beautiful," he added firmly.

"And the little dancer with the six curtains is your daughter," said the sandy man.

"Mais non," said Stroganoff astounded. "Why you think that?"

CHAPTER XIV

The opening night.

In ten minutes the curtain would be going up on an evening of all surpassing triumph.

Or would it?

At any rate, most of the costumes had come. And if the audience streaming in lacked the glow of the balletomane entering his taken-for-granted heaven, the Maryinsky, at any rate it was streaming, and, which was curious, bringing its children.

"Can it be," said General Dumka, gazing at the milling foyer, "that they have mistaken the date?"

"Impossible," said Stroganoff. "My friend, you make me laugh. To confuse the circus with the ballet! No, this cannot happen."

He gazed at a group of children, babbling and tugging at the folds of their mother's skirt. Doubt seized him. Soon it became a certainty. The children were howling their heads off and the mother was demanding her money back.

"See," said General Dumka in macabre triumph.

"Poof!" said Stroganoff.

They were fast reaching the stage where their nerves

were getting the better of them and making them want to get the better of one another.

Stroganoff proceeded to restore his morale by gazing at the crowded foyer. Why you could not see the marble staircase for medals and sables.

"Look!" said General Dumka. There was awe in his voice.

For the crowd was making way for a well-known black figure with a single lock of white hair and his habitual cortège of lofty followers.

Diaghilev and his disciples had come to the opening.

"It is a great honour," whispered General Dumka, "and also," he admitted, "a big surprise."

"What more natural than that one impresario should come to the opening of another," said Stroganoff casually. But his chest had already swollen out.

The cortège advanced. Stroganoff waited expectantly. The cortège swept by.

"What he say to me?" asked Stroganoff anxiously.

"He nodded," said Dumka. "Be satisfied."

Bowing gravely the cortège kept on its unsmiling way.

★　　★　　★

Backstage all was frenzy. Never had so many costumes arrived at the last moment. Never had there been such a last minute of frantic hammering, lost wreaths, mislaid mascots, and nervy mamoushkas commanding maddened daughters to keep calm.

For that matter never before had there been a wedged-into-a-corner elephant.

"Ten minutes," sang the call-boy.

"Mr. Stroganoff!" A strung-up mamoushka planted herself firmly in the bobbing about impresario's path. "In Omsk you promised . . ."

"Later," said Stroganoff. "To-morrow," he soothed her, "I promise you the row colossal."

He hurried on. Dancers plucked at his sleeve, electricians held out appealing hands, Nicholas Nevajno ducked behind him to avoid wishing his best friend luck. But Stroganoff forged purposefully ahead. He was the father of his family and he must bless his children.

First the little wife.

"Ah, c'est toi," said the mamoushka resigned, and she picked up her needle and went on with the ballet-skirt.

"My six curtains?" said Natasha, a porcelain angel in all save voice. . . .

*   *   *

The conductor rapped his baton. Silence fell on the house. In the background an elephant trumpeted.

A tremor passed down the spine of a pale little boy whose dark brows met. Leonide Massine had been brought to what his mamoushka thought was the circus. But somehow already he wasn't disappointed.

In his box Diaghilev was slightly out of mood. Nijinsky at home with a feverish cold and the provincial's curtain about to go up a bare ten minutes late. He hoped his own would be as punctual when he opened in Paris.

"Little Ginsberg," he told Bolm, "has not answered my wire. Bankers are slow, slow, slow."

"Bankers," said the dancer Bolm, not interested.

The house lights went down.

"Sylvia!" said Nicholas Nevajno contemptuously. He sought for further opprobrium. "Sylvia!" he found.

The footlights came up bathing the crimson curtains of the great proscenium in their ruby glow. In the dark sea of the auditorium noble bosoms rose a little and military backs stiffened. It was the Ballet. It might be from Omsk, but it was still the Ballet.

The conductor raised his baton. Delibes' beguiling music welled up.

The Company Stroganoff had opened in the Capital.

*　　*　　*

"The orchestra could be worse," said P. Puthyk, always eager to be pleased.

They listened.

"I deny this," said Stravinsky before long.

The curtain became a glade. The glade became infested with nymphs, fauns, and villagers. The statue of love became Arenskaya.

"What a pity she has left the Maryinsky," said Puthyk. "She has," he sought for the word, "personality."

"Personality possibly," said Fokine. He left it at that.

On the stage the simple story leapt, rotated and pattered on its way. The music charmed the house; it was sweet, it was soporific, it was disarming. Dowagers nodded approvingly and Grand Dukes waved cigarette-holders. Stroganoff had chosen wisely after all.

"Who is that?" asked Diaghilev as a Dresden china Sylvia sported by the brook.

"It is the wife of the director," said Nouvel. "Natasha Stroganova."

"The odalisk from Omsk," said Stravinsky.

"She could be better," said Fokine critically.

"But she could be worse," said Diaghilev. He made a note.

In the auditorium old military backs were nodding heads approvingly and young military backs were twirling moustaches.

"Elle est ravissante."

"Delicious."

"A second Trefilova."

The simple story seethed, bounced and overbalanced. The stage was full again of bounding, twirling figures.

"That one," said Diaghilev, gazing at an energetically rotating faun, "that one is no . . ." he paused and corrected himself. "Bolm," he substituted.

★   ★   ★

The simple story trundled on its complicated way. Presently it was the first interval.

Stroganoff, torn between pride and protest, roamed the crowded foyer, straining and craning to overhear those all-important, lightly thrown comments that his offering to the capital was bringing out. He was followed by a straining and craning General Dumka.

"I would never have believed it possible," said a Grand Duke with a monocle to a Grand Duke without one.

Stroganoff and Dumka exchanged glances.

"They are in ecstasy," they assured one another.

"The little Sylvia is charming." A young guardsman was twirling his moustache.

"Delicious," agreed his companion. He kissed his fingers.

The husband and impresario glowed.

"I have asked her to supper," said the guardsman.

The husband stopped glowing.

"Come," said General Dumka. "Let us have a drink."

"He has asked my Natasha to supper," said Stroganoff thickly. "I challenge him to a duel."

He took a step forward. Dumka pulled him back.

"Come," he said, "a little drink. What," he soothed, "is an invitation to supper? It does not follow," he argued, "that she will accept."

⋆　　⋆　　⋆

The Ballet Sylvia. Act II.

The simple story was growing more complicated every moment. In his stage box Aliosha had clasped his hands over his stomach. In spite of this it was still heaving.

"Where," he demanded indignantly as his son's bald dome came bobbing in, "where is my Katusha? Already it is Act II, and I have not seen her yet."

"She is waiting to take the house by storm in her temple," said Stroganoff comfortably. "The rest of the ballet," he waved it away, "is but the build-up."

Aliosha glowered at him. "It is not right that you tuck my Katusha in a temple where she is not seen till," he consulted his programme, "scene eleven."

"Nine," said Stroganoff.

"Now you juggle me the figures," said Aliosha crossly. "Tell me," he became the business-man, "how much money you lose this evening?"

"Papoushka," Stroganoff looked hurt. "Sois raisonable. To-night is the night of my triumph. I have invite all the capital and they have come and," he spread his hands, "they enjoy themselves." He waited hopefully for the roar of applause that should have greeted the end of the man who was no Nijinsky's solo.

One or two people did clap.

"Voilà," said Stroganoff making the best of it.

"But how much money you lose?" asked Aliosha stubbornly.

Stroganoff sighed. "It is not what we lose to-night that matter. It is how much we have left for to-morrow. It is of this that we must talk."

"Very well," said Aliosha. "How much then have we left for to-morrow?"

Stroganoff pondered. "Nothing," he said.

"So," said Aliosha. "So," he said ominously.

"It is not this that worry me," said Stroganoff. "It is the money for the next production, the new creation by Nevajno, that will draw all Petersburg and make me, Vladimir Stroganoff, the most talked-of impresario in," he considered, "the universe," he finished modestly.

"How much it cost?" asked Aliosha.

Stroganoff considered again. "Already it cost twice what we estimate in Omsk," he revealed, "and we only begin. So you see, my papoushka, I must have the finance."

"Nu?" said the papoushka unmoved.

"You must help me," said Stroganoff. "To-morrow," he coaxed, "my little father will write to my little grandfather and ask him for fifty-thousand roubles, or better," he amended, "sixty."

Up went the hands. "Dear God," said Aliosha, "that I should have a son who thinks his little grandfather will risk his own money. Aie! Aie! Aie!" He blew his nose.

"But the little grandfather is rich," said Stroganoff.

"The little grandfather is rich," said Aliosha severely, "because he does not do the good turn with his own money but only the money of others. That is the method practical. He will give you no more—may he live long in this world to bless us."

"May he live long," agreed Stroganoff dully. "Your own investments," he changed the subject, "they do well—no?"

"Sssh!" said Aliosha sternly. He pointed to the stage.

* * *

Act III.

The simple rural story had got too complicated to follow. Arenskaya had elbowed in a solo and a pas-de-deux. But at last Katusha was in her temple and Aliosha was leaning forward in his box and wondering if she was going to be allowed to step out of it.

But Vladimir Stroganoff was deep in conversation in the bar. He was talking to the comfortably stomached stranger of the Trans-Siberian Express.

The first ecstatic greetings were over. The stranger had congratulated Stroganoff on his triumphant opening. Stroganoff had congratulated the stranger on his presence at it.

The stranger had sympathized with the absence of the little grandfather. Stroganoff had wished the little grandfather a long life and poofed him away. They had had the little drink, they had had the other little drink, and at the third little drink the conversation had taken a serious turn.

. . . "This little Baskova in Vladivostok," said the stranger, "is—how to put it—my discovery."

"Entendu," said Stroganoff.

"It is not right," said the stranger, "that she should bury her talent in there."

"Bien sûr," said Stroganoff, temples in which to tuck her already floating in his mind.

"But," the stranger shook a worried head, "here, in the capital, it is not easy to arrange for the début of a ballerina."

"It is not easy," Stroganoff agreed.

"But it must be arranged," said the stranger warmly. "For if the little Baskova comes to the capital and I have nothing for her, she—how to put it—will have nothing for me."

"It is not impossible to arrange," said Stroganoff. "But it is . . . expensive."

The stranger fiddled with his watch-chain.

"I am not a rich man," he said.

"Me too, I am now poor," said Stroganoff.

They looked at one another. Each understood the other perfectly.

"And so," Stroganoff told the sandy man, "I find my first backer. And as it was in the beginning so it has been ever since."

"Has it?" said the sandy man.

The simple story had come to an end. Or at least it had stopped going on. The artists were lined up to take their curtain.

The first curtain was all that a curtain should be. For one thing it came down slowly and gave the artists plenty of time to bow radiantly to the house and politely to one another. And the house, if it did not rise at them, at least applauded politely. After all, the capital had seen worse companies than this—in the provinces.

The second curtain, according to plan, went to the soloists. The applause was a little warmer—more personal. A great deal of noise came from the stage-box to which the Goddess Diane was bowing.

The third curtain belonged to the delicious Stroganova, to Arenskaya—all personality, and to the man who was no Nijinsky.

The audience still applauded.

The fourth curtain went to Natasha alone. They brought on her bouquets. They brought on the basket of orchids higher than herself. They placed it in front of her.

Diaghilev went. So did Benois, Fokine, Stravinsky, Bolm and Nouvel; P. Puthyk sat on applauding.

The fifth curtain showed Natasha in front of her company. The applause still survived, but there wasn't much to spare.

As it ended Stroganoff came rushing out of the bar.

"How many curtains?" he panted.

"Five," said a general. He shrugged.

"Ah," said Stroganoff. He fixed his eyes on the tab and held his hands ready.

The curtains were parting. His wife, his little angel, was coming out. What a moment for a husband! Stroganoff closed his eyes.

On the stage, behind the about-to-part curtains, Natasha, flushed and palpitating, listened acutely to what was left of the applause.

"Six curtains for Stroganova," she breathed.

In the wings the mamoushka crossed herself.

The stage director gave the signal. Natasha smoothed her frock, switched on her stage radiance, and moved towards the narrow lane that would bring her out in front of the tabs.

"Six curtains," she breathed, and, stumbling over Arenskaya's outstretched foot, measured her length on the stage.

"Brava," shouted Stroganoff. "Brava!" And he stamped and applauded with all his might.

"But, my darling," said Arenskaya. "I am desolated. But what could I do? There were you on the floor, your face all dirty from the dust, your costume—mh, mh, mh! And there was the audience waiting—you could not face them like that. It break my heart, but what could I do? I had to save the day. The public were waiting to applaud. I had to take your curtain for you."

"You showed great presence of mind, darling," said Natasha.

They kissed.

The worried-to-death Stroganoff, hurrying into his wife's dressing-room, blinked.

"You are the friends?" he asked amazed.

"But the friends bosom," said Arenskaya. She blew the purpling mamoushka a kiss and withdrew.

Stroganoff opened his arms. "My darling," he said thankfully.

"Your darling—poof!" said Natasha. "You sack that woman to-morrow or I never speak to you again."

"To-night," said the mamoushka.

"My six curtains," said Natasha. "My six curtains of which I have dreamt, eaten, and slept, my six curtains in the capital—ruined! And," she turned on him, "it is all your fault for bringing that wicked woman to the company."

"My darling infant," said Stroganoff patiently. "Sois raisonable. Is it her fault that you fall down at the moment critical?"

"Yes," said Natasha.

"Yes," said the mamoushka.

They were agreed.

"She trip me up," screamed Natasha. "She stick out her foot as I go forward." She fell upon Stroganoff and pummelled his dress shirt. "Do you hear, Vladimir? She trip me up."

Stroganoff seized the fighting little hands and summoned all his tact as he wrestled.

"She will be put in her place that one," he promised. "To-night I have arranged for a new ballerina to come to the company."

Natasha stopped wrestling. Temperaments could wait. This was serious.

"A new ballerina?" she said.

"A new ballerina!" said the mamoushka sharply.

"The ballerina beauteous from Vladivostok," said Stroganoff. He waited for the chorus of congratulation.

"Villain," said Natasha. "Monster. So already you plan to be unfaithful."

This reminded Stroganoff of something.

"Unfaithful," he said. "Me! What of the invitation to supper that you get from the young guardsman at whom no doubt," he accused, "you make the eyes from the stage or never would he have had the courage to ask."

"One guardsman," said Natasha scornfully. She snatched a batch of visiting cards from her dressing-table and threw them in Stroganoff's face. "I have six invitations from guardsmen. And one from an Admiral." She threw it.

Anger left Stroganoff. He became anxious.

"My darling," he said, "you have not accepted one of them?"

Natasha tossed her head. "On the contrary," she said, "I have accepted them all."

She snatched up her fur coat and strode into the corridor.

The mamoushka ran out after her.

"Natasha, " she wailed. "Come back. You are but in your corset."

CHAPTER XV

C<small>LASS.</small>

But not at the Maryinsky.

There was an assortment of tunics and tights. They did not match. There was a piano. It was not in tune. There was a small group of onlookers. They had no right to be there, and the least they might do was pay attention. There was a lion-tamer. He was watching the teacher. There was a teacher. She was wishing she was a lion-tamer. How to correct the wife of the management without losing her job at once?

"Not like this, chérie," she said. "So."

She waited anxiously. She relaxed. She was still on the salary list. Natasha had shot her a look, but she had obeyed.

"Beautiful, my darling," said the once divine Korovina. "The head a little higher—so."

"So," said Arenskaya helpfully from a corner. She demonstrated. Natasha refused to look.

Stroganoff came in. He beamed at the teacher who smiled at him. He beamed at Natasha who scowled at him. He ignored Arenskaya who winked at him. He crossed over to General Dumka and embraced him.

"We are the success triumphant," he announced. "For the

129

next performance already two boxes are booked."

"What did I tell you," said Dumka overjoyed. He opened his arms. Now that the first night *crise* was over, the desire of the two friends to contradict each other had been replaced by a determination to agree with anything the other might say. "We are the success. Everyone come to us. Except," he remembered, "Trefilova. She admire the turquoise hatpin, but she say 'no.'"

"You take back the hatpin?" asked Stroganoff anxiously.

"Hélas!" Dumka shrugged, "it is already in her hat." He turned to brighter topics. "The notices," he said, "could be worse."

They discussed them while Madame Korovina conducted the class gently through little hoops of peril. What would Johansen have said of that pirouette? She shrugged the thought off.

"Concentrate a little, my darling," she said. "Finish in position. You are not," she risked it, "in a circus." She looked at the lion-tamer. She wished she hadn't. "Two turns," she exhorted, "and finish facing M'sieur le Directeur."

Katusha tried again.

But M'sieur le Directeur was juggling with a sheaf of notices.

"Pas mal," he flicked. "Pas mal du tout." He flicked again. His face fell.

Inevitably, irrevocably, irretrievably he had come to the column signed Valerien Svetlov.

"Take no notice of that one," said Dumka consolingly. "It is well known that he likes nothing."

Stroganoff scowled like a disappointed schoolboy. "But he should not raise the hopes," he complained. "To begin with the praise faint. . . . 'Omsk is to be congratulated for one thing!' . . . naturally I think it is my ballet, n'est ce pas?"

"Si, si," said Dumka.

"But it appears later," said Stroganoff moodily, "it is because my ballet has left."

"Poof!" said Dumka.

"Tiens," said Stroganoff. A slight figure stood hesitating in the doorway. "Where have I seen that one before?"

"With Diaghilev," said Dumka impressed.

Smiling politely, P. Puthyk advanced into the room. Arenskaya, who had not been paying much attention to the teacher, stopped attending altogether. She came out to the front of the class and proceeded unasked to do a few solo steps of which she was very sure. The teacher, behind a carefully non-committal face, was wondering whether to say anything. Natasha, behind a china shepherdess smile, was composing sentences to say later.

Puthyk bowed faultlessly to Korovina.

"Mille pardons, Madame," he said, "that I interrupt your class, but I have come with a message for Mademoiselle Stroganova."

"Entendu, M'sieur Puthyk," said Korovina. "Mon ange," she beckoned, "viens ici un moment."

Arenskaya came forward.

"My congratulations," said Puthyk, "on your admirable performance."

Arenskaya bowed low. By the time she came up again

Puthyk was whispering with Natasha while an apprehensive Stroganoff had hovered himself as near as he dared which was still not near enough to overhear.

"But at once," said Natasha. She dropped a brief curtsey vaguely in the direction of the teacher and made off.

"Your wife," Puthyk told Stroganoff, "is a very talented dancer. She will go far."

"Yes," said Stroganoff anxiously, "but where?"

But Puthyk must have been deaf, for he had hurried away and already was out of earshot.

"I wonder where I shall lunch to-day," mused Arenskaya audibly.

*　　*　　*

"Assez de désespoir," said Sergei Diaghilev. "We have been ruined before. There is no need to be depressed about it."

"But it is getting monotonous," said Stravinsky.

Outside the sun was shining. Inside Diaghilev's apartment the great draperies were drawn and all the lights were on. Diaghilev hated daylight. He admitted its inevitability, but it depressed him. So did little Ginsberg's letter lying on his desk.

"The man is never satisfied," grumbled Benois. "We bring him the success artistic and 'e wants to make the money too."

"Or at least not lose too much," said Nouvel fairly.

They ignored him.

"He is a business-man," said Fokine. "You shouldn't have shown him the figures. It was not the moment."

"It is very important this moment when you wish to raise the hurricane," Stroganoff explained to the sandy man. "You pick it right and—poof! you are the millionaire. You pick it wrong and—biff!" he jabbed his thumb, "you are in the bortsch. So you will understand, my friend, that the choosing of this moment is an art to which an impresario must give much attention."

"I'm beginning to gather that," said the sandy man.

"But, croyez moi," said Stroganoff, "there are many impresarios in London to-day who do not realize this. Because the backer he keep singing that he is a business-man, they think it is business that he comes here to do. And they prepare for him the figures elaborate and they talk to him of the house capacity, and the number of matinées, and the get-in and the get-out, and many many things that do not fascinate the business-man at all. And the business-man he see that he can only do in the theatre what he can do with less hazard in the city—mooch less—and he go away. And it serve them right," said Stroganoff severely, "for that is no way to treat a business-man."

"H'm," said the sandy man.

"Me," said Stroganoff, "I play the business-man like a fish."

"A poor fish," said the sandy man.

"I cast the bait," said Stroganoff, "I twiddle up and down, I let him run away and I pull him back and presently—poof—he is in the net, and what is more," he waggled a finger, "happy to be in it. For some time at least," he conceded. "But I bore you perhaps?"

"No, no," said the sandy man. "Please go on."

Stroganoff beamed.

"So," he continued, "when I seek to bait my hook I do not dwell on figures for then he would wish to inspect them and it does not do, my friend, to have your backers inspect your figures until too late. But also I am careful to save his pride. Each time he sing he is a business-man, I tell him the figures will be ready to-morrow, and I talk to him of our triumphant season in the Argentine. And it was," he said in awe. "We show a profit." He looked at Pavlova for confirmation. "And then," he said, "I take the rich one to lunch, and I pay for it, for there is nothing pleases the rich one so much as to be given the little lunch by someone else. And I take him to rehearsal but not for too long, and I invite him to my box, and I give for him the little party backstage, where his wife does not come, and where he drink too mooch gin and all the choryphées call him uncle. And presently, if he can still stand, he make the speech. Ah! those speeches!" Stroganoff shuddered. "And after that," he finished, "he give me the cheque and our season is guarantee."

"As simple as that," said the sandy man.

"It is simple," said Stroganoff. "You must remember only to keep the business-man away from your figures. You must remember it all the time for, if he sees them, he will fear, not the loss, but that you may think he is not a good business-man. Save the backer's pride," pronounced Stroganoff, "and you can ruin him all you wish and he will thank you for doing it. The chi-chi," he summed it up, "it is important. But not to see the figures, that, my friend, it is vital."

"You shouldn't have let him see the figures," said Bolm. "He is a business-man."

Diaghilev swept back his white lock with an abstracted hand. "Where do I go for money now?" he brooded.

"To the State," said Benois.

"It is a pity you were not more polite to Teleyakov," said Nouvel. He shook his head.

"Politeness would not help," said Diaghilev. "The State is jealous of me, do you not understand? They think I take the réclame that is the due of their theatres and that I steal their best dancers and there," he chuckled suddenly, "they are right."

"Money, money," said Benois. "Always it is money that holds us back."

"Where can I get some ballet shoes?" mused Nijinsky. "Teleyakov maybe?" He tasted the idea. "Not Teleyakov," he decided.

"Certainly not Teleyakov," said Fokine. "He is our enemy."

"I will write to little Ginsberg again," decided Diaghilev. "I will tell him," he paused to crystallize the concept, "I will tell him that he must do what he cannot do." He gulped his lemon tea.

"Tell him to find a little grandfather," said Stravinsky.

P. Puthyk hurried in.

"She is here," he announced importantly.

"Who," said the company crossly.

"The porcelain doll from Omsk," said Puthyk. "She ask questions all the way. But I tell her nothing," he assured them.

"I will see her," said Diaghilev.

Fokine looked interested. "You are making her an offer?"

"Why not?" said Diaghilev. "She has chic. She will please Paris."

"But her husband," said Stravinsky. "Will he be pleased?"

"Her husband." Diaghilev went behind his face. "I do not understand you, my friend. I do not understand you at all."

★ ★ ★

It was 2.15 at the little restaurant round the corner. Russian dancers lunch late. The room was buzzing with conversation. The usual conversation. "My public."

"In class I . . ."

"That conductor."

"My mamoushka says . . ." floated from the pouting lips of every divinity in the room.

Save one.

This divinity was looking definitely thoughtful. She had to tell her husband something and he wasn't going to like it. The husband was thoughtful, too. He had to tell his wife something and she was going to loathe it.

"The bortsch is cold," said Natasha to pass the time. How to tell him that she had been offered a European tour —with Diaghilev?

"But the champagne is warm," said Stroganoff postponing the inevitable. How to tell her he'd been offered a new ballet with the little Baskova dancing the lead?

The proprietor wandered up. "Everything as you like it?" he enquired.

"Delicious," they assured him vaguely.

Relieved, the proprietor wandered away.

"Vladimir," said Natasha, pushing aside her untouched plate. "What is the dearest thing in the world to you?"

This was easy. "But you, my darling," said Stroganoff. "All day, all night, I plan for you. Everything that I do is for your happiness. I promise you that I will make you the greatest ballerina in the world only . . . only," he hesitated, "not all at once."

"Vladimir," said Natasha. "I have been given a great opportunity."

"But not all at once," repeated Stroganoff, who had not been listening. "Sometimes it is the policy to draw back a little from the public so that they clamour for you all the more. To give the limelight to some" he waved a disparaging hand, "to some lesser dancer so that when you return they realize what they have been missing." He brightened a little. That was well put, he reflected. Tactful.

"He said I had chic," said Natasha, who had not been listening.

"So," said Stroganoff, "I have found the backer with much money with the little protégée with not too much talent."

"Four hundred francs a month," said Natasha. "It is not the money—it is the opportunity."

"And," said Stroganoff, "the little Baskova signs her contract to-morrow."

It was out. Or part of it. And Natasha, who had caught the word "Contract," was now all attention.

"Who sign what?" she asked sharply.

"But the little Baskova," said Stroganoff. "I sign her for the new Nevajno, and," he gulped, "she dance the lead."

It was out. All of it.

"So," said Natasha. The mouth tightened.

"It is only so that the public clamour for you the more," Stroganoff hurried on. "And also," he admitted, "because without the backer I have no money to put it on."

"So," said Natasha. "So. The little Baskova is to dance the lead while I . . ." She fought for words to express her indignation. And as she fought she remembered.

"Never mind, my darling," she said with such sweetness that the tensed Stroganoff almost reeled. "No doubt she will do well enough. . . . And also Arenskaya will be livid."

"You are not cross," said Stroganoff dazed. "You do not intend to scratch out my eyes?"

"But why, my darling," said Natasha. "I know that you study only my interests and I know also that money it is important, and if you think that it is right that the little Baskova dance the lead then it must be so."

"But it is an angel," burst out Stroganoff. "A veritable angel." In his relief he drank her champagne. "What other ballerina would be so reasonable? If we were not in public I would embrace you." He tried.

"Then all is well," said Natasha. "You put on the Nevajno with the little Baskova. You have the success—I hope. And when I am back from Europe I lead the company again."

"Si, si," said Stroganoff. "Comment! Quoi donc! What the 'ell?"

"Europe, my darling," said Natasha. She sighed. "I was worried at leaving you, Vladimir, but now I see that it fits in very well with your plans."

"Comment!" said Stroganoff. "Quoi!"

"I see Diaghilev this morning," said Natasha.

"Diaghilev!" said Stroganoff. "Qu'est ce que tu me chantes?"

"He makes me the offer," said Natasha. "The offer to go to Europe." Now for it. "I accept."

Stroganoff leapt to his feet. "I kill him," he announced. He looked round for an implement and found a fish-knife. Brandishing it wildly, he rushed out.

"Valerien says," said Trefilova.

"The conductor . . ." said Kyasht.

"My mamoushka . . ." said Karsavina.

"My mamoushka!" remembered Natasha. She burst into tears and stumbled out of the restaurant.

They will be back to-morrow, thought the proprietor philosophically.

He put away the bill.

★ ★ ★

"And so, my dear Ginsberg," the purple ink was spidering its way across the page, "I am in no mood to hear of stock markets, short credits and unfortunate speculations."

Diaghilev passed his hand over his white lock. He crossed out "unfortunate."

A bald head hurtled into the room. It was the man from Omsk. He was brandishing a fish-knife. Diaghilev looked up in some annoyance. Had he not told his servant he did not wish to be disturbed.

"Good afternoon," he said to the waving knife. "Your appointment was at . . . ?" He looked at his engagement book where he knew the afternoon would be blank. "I trust I have not kept you waiting."

"Villain," shouted Stroganoff uncrushed. "You wish to steal my wife. Despoiler! Schemer! Cheat!"

"Not despoiler," said Diaghilev.

"I come to demand the explanation." Stroganoff thrust out his chin. "I get it quick or else . . ." Failing to find the threat he brandished the fish-knife.

"Behave yourself," said Diaghilev sharply. "You are not in Omsk. Sit down."

Stroganoff gulped. He decided he could be just as defiant seated. The armchair was vast and deep. He was sunk.

"Sir," said Diaghilev. "To cut this unexpected interview short I propose to answer your questions before you can ask them. Before you can ask them," he repeated sternly and the struggling up Stroganoff sank down again.

"I have made one of your dancers an offer," said Diaghilev. He held up his hand. "One of your dancers," he repeated. "She will accept it." He held up his hand again. "You have made offers to many of my dancers. They have not accepted."

Stroganoff shifted restlessly in the deep armchair. He put the fish-knife in his pocket. It was uncomfortable. He took it out again.

"I have approached Mademoiselle Stroganova," said Diaghilev, "because she has charm and will please Paris, and her dancing is, enfin, not too bad. This to me is a sufficient reason to engage a dancer. Nothing else is my concern."

"But me, it is my concern," burst out the pent-up Stroganoff. "It is my wife that you take to Paris."

"Yes?" said Diaghilev unmoved.

Stroganoff levered himself up. He resolved to speak calmly.

"Voleur!" he shouted. "Tyrant! Monopolist! All, all you want for yourself. You want all the dancers? All the designers, all the musicians . . ."

"That is so," said Diaghilev.

"You want all the Nijinskys . . ."

"That too," said Diaghilev.

"You will not permit anyone to live. Ever since I come from Omsk, every trouble, every crisis—it is you. I approach an artist—you have her. I seek the long-term credit—it is yours. I commission an orchestration and the composer he break off in the middle to orchestrate for you . . ." He ran out of breath.

"If I were in Omsk," said Diaghilev, polite but deadly, "no doubt the process would be reversed."

"You pay with the promises," Stroganoff almost wept. "And me, me—I have to pay with the cash and must plead with my little grandfather to get it."

"The little grandfather," mused Diaghilev, "is in Petersburg?"

"Non!" said Stroganoff forcibly. "Never, never, shall you get the little grandfather. Never, never shall you lure my Natasha. I will argue with her. I will plead with her. I will promise her all that you can give her." He pointed the fish-knife. "And more!"

"Paris?" asked Diaghilev.

"That, too," said Stroganoff. "I can promise it—yes."

Diaghilev spread his hands. "In that case," he said, "I must not detain you."

Stroganoff brightened. "You withdraw your offer?" He asked hopefully.

"You will have much to do arranging a European tour at such short notice."

"But my wife . . ." said Stroganoff.

Diaghilev shrugged. "The dancer will choose which offer she prefers."

"You wish to separate us?" said Stroganoff passionately, "and we are married but six months—next week."

"You can come with her," said Diaghilev. "I do not refuse to travel the husbands."

"But my company . . ." said Stroganoff.

"Your company?" said Diaghilev. "How can your company possibly concern me?"

He rose. Stroganoff found himself ushered to the door.

"Good day," said Diaghilev. "Should you wish to see me again, please make an appointment. I should be most distressed if I were out."

"That is a lie," said Stroganoff defiantly.

But he said it to the closed door.

It opened.

"Your knife?" said Diaghilev courteously. He bowed. The door closed again.

"Yes, my friend," Stroganoff told the sandy man. "I tell the great Diaghilev what I think of him. I speak freely my mind—never has he been tell off so well. And when I leave he is crush. Crush!" He thumped the desk.

"But all the same," he admitted, "me, I am a little crush too."

★   ★   ★

"My darling," said the mamoushka, "let us remember we are reasonable women. Six curtains are important. But Paris," she gloated, "Paris is more important."

"He promised them to me," said Natasha mutinously. "At least he said—'all things are possible.' And now he has not put it in the contract. It is no use, mamoushka, I cannot trust Diaghilev."

They were sitting in mamoushka's bedroom and mamoushka was brushing the hair of her daughter. For, naturally, at this crisis in her life, Natasha had gone back to mother, leaving her husband in another bedroom in the same hotel, frantic and definitely alone.

"My darling," said mamoushka. "Let us remember we are realists. Let us quietly consider what is the worst that can happen if you sign this contract. We open in Paris and you do not have your six curtains. Hélas! But," she pointed to the bright side, "you have had the success enormous—

this is inevitable—and Karsavina she is livid. And after we work on Diaghilev, you and I—but more I than you. We plead, we threaten, we take out our false teeth . . . Diaghilev is but a man like the others. Look," she said, "what we have done with Vladimir."

"Poor Vladimir," said Natasha.

The house 'phone burbled. Natasha crossed to the wall, unhooked the receiver and squeezed.

"My darling," said Stroganoff in an adenoidal croak. "Come back to me, I beseech. Without you I cannot sleep."

"Useless to entreat," said Natasha coldly. "After the things you shout to me through the dressing-room door to-night I have left you for ever."

She stopped squeezing and hung up.

"It is not only the six curtains," she told mamoushka. "But what does Diaghilev offer me in the contract? In Giselle I am a Wili. In Swan Lake I dance the Queen only if Karsavina and Lopokova are ill, and Spessitzeva and Kshessinskaya cannot be there in time—and then only if the programme it is not changed."

"You have a solo," said mamoushka.

"One solo!" said Natasha. "And in what? Les Sylphides. A novelty that will not last a season! Already they use it as a throwaway to open the performance. No, no," she decided, "I stay where I am."

The house 'phone burbled violently. Natasha advanced on it, unhooked and squeezed.

"Mais, my darling," pleaded Stroganoff. "Is it my fault that I shout?—you would not open the door."

"I will not open the door," said Natasha. "I will not

open my arms. I will not dance in your company again—never, never, never."

"But, my darling. Consid . . ."

Natasha had stopped squeezing.

"My darling," said mamoushka. "Remember we are women who do not act on impulse. We know well how to look into the future, us, and how to await our moment. We are newcomers to the company as," she reminded her, "we were newcomers to Omsk. And look what we achieved there."

"Non," said Natasha violently. "I will not marry Diaghilev."

Mamoushka waved the hairbrush.

"Some men," she explained, "it is necessary to marry. Others—no. What is this new ballet they are talking of?"

" 'Carnaval,' " said Natasha. "Me, I understudy Papillon."

The house telephone exploded.

"But this is impossible," said the mamoushka as she advanced.

"My darling," groaned Stroganoff. "I cannot sleep."

"Me neither," snapped the mamoushka. She stopped squeezing.

"Poor Vladimir." Natasha softened. "He does his best for me. Perhaps I am unkind."

"A daughter of mine unkind!" said the mamoushka incredulously. "The hour is late and I am fatigued. Your career I will discuss, but this nonsense . . ." She waved it away. "To bed," she said briskly.

They settled in side by side.

"The morning brings its own counsel," said mamoushka, "so let us·leave our project in God's good hands till then."

"In God's good hands," agreed Natasha piously. "All the same," she plumped her pillow, "if Vladimir had any sense he would come and fetch me."

There was a timid knock at the door. Natasha and mamoushka looked at each other.

The door edged open. A bald dome peered round.

"Ah, my two little pigeons!" said Stroganoff falsely. "In bed already!" He beamed.

They looked at him.

"What a pretty picture you make." Stroganoff took a tentative step forward, making a pretty good picture himself in a plum-coloured dressing-gown on inside out and only one bedroom slipper. He looked anxiously at Natasha's face for the trace of a welcoming smile. It didn't seem to be there. "The pretty picture," he repeated, and took another step.

"Charming," he said, "the conseille de famille. The little daughter who would fly away before the wings are set," he crept forward, "and the little mother who understands where her real future lies." He looked at the unyielding granite face before him and took two more quick steps.

"A conseille de famille," he shook his head, "and the little papoushka excluded. No, no, my children, it is not right—this." In a little rush he sat down on the edge of the bed.

"Go away," said Natasha. "How dare you come here after all the things that you have said to me. I have left you for ever. Go away! Go away!" She threw a pillow at him and burst into tears.

"There," said the mamoushka well pleased. "See what you have done."

Stroganoff clutched the pillow. He looked at mamoushka's night-capped head. If he felt an impulse he restrained it.

"Nu," he said. "I am the clumsy business-man. The wicked ogre. The hard-hearted husband—isn't it?"

"You, you, you," sobbed Natasha. She flung her arms round him.

Stroganoff clutched. "See what I have done," he said triumphantly. "There, there, there."

Mamoushka sniffed. "You are standing in the way of my daughter's career," she said. "That's what you are doing."

"I can give her all Diaghilev can and more," proclaimed Stroganoff aroused. "I will take her to Paris. To London. I will present her at Covent Garden. And she shall not," he made an inspired guess, "have the two small solos and the understudy. She shall have . . ."

"Six curtains," sobbed Natasha.

"Bien sûr," said Stroganoff. "It will be in the contract."

Natasha dried her eyes. "When we go?"

"But at once," said Stroganoff. "Only first we must finish the season and then we are rich."

Mamoushka sniffed.

"Mais si," said Stroganoff. "Did you not count the house to-night. We lose only five hundred roubles—almost the profit," he boasted.

Mamoushka sniffed again.

"The new Nevajno ballet," said Stroganoff undaunted, "it will be the sensation, our prestige it soar, and the Government it give us the backing. Already," he swanked, "I am the comrades bosom with best friend of Teleyakov. Soon all will be arranged."

"My little husband," said Natasha. She climbed out of bed and put on her dressing-gown. She remembered something. "The little Baskova," she said, and climbed back again.

"The little Baskova?" The mamoushka clutched at the new straw. "Who is she?"

"She is from Vladivostok," said Natasha. "Vladimir has rashly promised her the new Nevajno but now," she looked all ready to get out of bed again, "he has changed his mind." She smiled winningly.

"The little Baskova," said Stroganoff, "brings the backing. She rehearses the ballet to-morrow." He raised his hand. "It does not follow my little calf and my little," he looked at the mamoushka, "cow, that she will dance it. It is a long way between the first rehearsal and the opening night, and," he put a finger to his nose, "many things can happen."

"You will sack her," ordered mamoushka.

"Me—no," said Stroganoff, "for if I did the backer will take away his money. But Nevajno," he comforted them, "is very hasty. He has quarrelled," he illustrated, "with his best friend. It is possible that he will quarrel with the little Baskova."

"These things can be arranged," said Natasha.

"Trust me," said Stroganoff. "All will be well."

Natasha considered. "And anyway," she mused, "Arenskaya will be livid."

"Go to bed—both of you," snapped the mamoushka. She knew when she had lost a battle.

CHAPTER XVI

Tʜʀᴇᴇ days later the little Baskova attended her first rehearsal. She was dreadful.

"Picture to yourself my embarrassment," Stroganoff told the sandy man. "On the one hand," he waved it, "I have the new ballet and the money. On the other," he waved that, "there is the little Baskova. It was not that I expected her to be the sensation, but she . . . was . . . a . . ."

"Little Baskova," supplied the sandy man helpfully.

"She is pretty enough," said Stroganoff. "She has the sex appeal. When she stand still it is not too bad. But when she dance—aie!" He threw up his hands. "It is clear at once that it is impossible she is a soloist in the capital."

"She'd want a solo," mused the sandy man. He was not thinking of the little Baskova.

"What to do?" Stroganoff went on. "I let her dance and my prestige it is the ruin. I give her sack and my bank balance it is the bust. I puzzle, I think, I argue, I tear my hair, and I am at the end of my wits. Until one day I am lunching with Arenskaya at the little restaurant round the corner . . . we are both a little distrait. . . ."

"The Grand Duke . . ." said Kshessinskaya.

"The Director," said Preobrajenskaya.

"The Wigmaker . . ." said Trefilova.

"My mamoushka . . ." said Karsavina.

"My shoes . . ." mourned Nijinsky.

The babble flowed on.

"Aie me," said Arenskaya.

"Aie me," said Stroganoff.

They put their heads on their elbows and ignored their coffee.

"My bill," called Diaghilev.

The proprietor brought it himself. He waited hopefully. But Diaghilev only signed.

No news from little Ginsberg yet, thought the proprietor stoically.

Stroganoff watched the hated cortège traverse to the door. How to snub sitting down? He turned a scorching glare on Diaghilev's oblivious back.

"The next time I see the villain face to face I tell him something," he assured Arenskaya.

But Arenskaya had not heard. Her eyes were on the cortège, Stravinsky, Benois, Bolm, Nijinsky, Fokine, Bakst, with P. Puthyk prancing importantly in the rear.

"Aie me," said Arenskaya, "I fear I shall marry with that one."

"He is your lover?" asked Stroganoff politely and not very interested.

"As yet he scarcely knows that I exist," said Arenskaya. "But he will marry me all the same. Aie me," she sighed, "it is very sad."

Stroganoff remembered that he was the father of his company. He shook off his own troubles and prepared to listen to Arenskaya's.

"A marriage between artists," he said doubtfully. "M'h. M'h. M'h."

"I know," said Arenskaya. "If I were wise I would marry a Grand Duke." She glanced at Kshessinskaya and raised her voice a little. "It is not too difficult."

"Or at least a banker," said Stroganoff toying with the idea of Abram of Omsk.

"Puthyk cannot help me in my career," said Arenskaya. "He is but the assistant to the assistant of the big Sergei Grigorieff. He is a good dancer and he has great sincerity. But he has no push. He cannot even scheme for himself. How then can he help me?"

"Then why marry him?" asked Stroganoff.

"I love him," said Arenskaya despairingly. "Voilà tout!"

"Poof," said Stroganoff. "The little affaire and all will be well."

"The little affaire I have with others," said Arenskaya. "Puthyk I will marry. You will see. I will be unfaithful to him, bien sûr, but I will never love anyone else. Hélas!" She sipped her coffee and the tears ran down her cheeks. "I am so young," she said, "but my fate is sealed. It would have been nice to have married just one Grand Duke."

Stroganoff looked for the bright side. "Maybe," he said, "Puthyk will not want to marry."

"He will," sobbed Arenskaya. "And it will be the happiest day of my life," she gulped defiantly.

At a corner table Nicholas Nevajno pulled out a pencil.

"I sign the bill," he said loftily.

The proprietor made an effort. "Mais, M'sieur . . ." he began.

"I sign," said Nevajno firmly. He scribbled and strode out.

From a table at the other corner of the room Nevajno's best friend glared after him and gave him a good two minutes' start. Then he beckoned the proprietor.

"My bill," he said. "I sign."

Arenskaya dabbed her eyes. "But enough of my troubles," she said. "Let us talk about yours."

"Me," said Stroganoff, "but I have no troubles at all. I have the new ballet—the money—what could trouble me?" He laughed. It didn't sound so good.

"The little Baskova," said Arenskaya, and Stroganoff was at once plunged in gloom.

"So you notice it too," he despaired.

"Mais voyons, Vladimir," said Arenskaya. "Am I not in class? Do I not watch rehearsals? Is it not evident to the whole world that she would not be there but for her chocolate papoushka?"

"Ah, so," said Stroganoff sadly. "It is as clear as that?"

"Vladimir," said Arenskaya earnestly, "I have all our good at heart. It is not because I want the rôle myself— though it would suit me well—that I tell you the little Baskova must not dance. Let Natasha have it." She waved an arm largely.

"My little pigeon is not as reasonable as usual at the moment," said Stroganoff. "Every day she gets the sweet- meats from Diaghilev and every night she makes me the

scene. And there is nothing I can do—nothing! No Baskova," he crystallized it, "no ballet."

"Are there not other rich men in the capital!" asked
Arenskaya.

"They have all got little Baskovas," said Stroganoff help-
lessly. "What will it profit me to change? I tell you, my
darling, that I and my brave Dumka are in despair. We
cannot plan, we cannot eat, and me, I have not slept for
three nights now." He pointed to the circles under his eyes.

Arenskaya was all sympathy. "There I can help you,"
she said. She took out a golden phial from her bag and
passed it across. "My sleeping draught," she said. "I have
no need for it now that I get acquainted with Nevajno's
best friend, the rascal!"

"It will put me to sleep?" asked Stroganoff.

"One little drop in a glass of milk," said Arenskaya, "and
you are asleep immediate for twelve hours. It is very
strong," she warned, "so do not take too much."

"Bon," said Stroganoff dutifully. He tucked the phial in
his pocket.

"And now," said Arenskaya, "it is time for me to keep
the rendezvous with your little wife. We are driving in
the Park together . . ."

"You blink, my friend," said Stroganoff to the sandy
man. "Arenskaya and my little pigeon the friends bosom
in the Park! But in the ballet this is natural."

"Is it indeed?" said the sandy man.

"It needs only a common enemy," said Stroganoff wisely,
"for the enemies deadly to become the friends immediate."

"The little Baskova," said the sandy man. "I see."

"But, while to defeat the common enemy they are the friends bosom," said Stroganoff, "there still goes on the rivalry, the lookout and the little schemes for the double cross. It is like," he sought for an example, "the nations united."

"I don't get you," said the sandy man coldly.

★　　★　　★

The little restaurant was empty. Stroganoff sat on thinking, thinking, thinking. Money to get the ballet on. Money to get the little Baskova off. Money to take Natasha to Europe. . . .

The proprietor came over with the bill. Resigned, he extended a pencil.

In his abstraction Stroganoff paid.

★　　★　　★

The new Nevajno creation.

At the moment it consisted of two lines of unsat-upon chairs—the cliffs of Dover. Several chalk marks—footlights, backcloth and wings. A piano—the orchestra. The conductor—himself. He was waving a conscientious wrist at the ignoring back of the pianist.

Rehearsals held in the classroom are always like this.

The creating genius, clad in a Russian tunic, torn under the arms, cotton tights, and dirty white ballet shoes, his black hair escaping from under a cerise bandeau, was working in a glow of satisfaction. Even his best friend stalking around and sniffing failed to revolt him. His new conception was taking shape, a rather peculiar shape—full of bulges and odd angles. Three people had called him "Maestro" and two of them had schanged him schmall scheque. He was going to play Baccarat to-night. What more could a choreographer want?

"Mlle. Baskova," he called. "Your entrée, if you would be so kind."

The little Baskova detached herself from her chocolate-papoushka and hipped her way to the wrong chalk mark.

The calm choreographer folded his arms. He resolved to speak gently.

"Little idiot," he hissed. "Do you still not know where to enter?"

The chocolate-papoushka flushed. "She was up late last night," he apologized to Dumka beside him.

"It makes little difference," said General Dumka non-committally.

They composed themselves to watch the slow unbirth of the masterpiece.

The piano churned. The conductor waved. The corps-de-ballet went into action—angular action. The chocolate-papoushka stroked his chin dubiously. Nobody *sur les pointes!* No kiss-the-fingers at the audience! No little pirouettes! What was this thing?

"It is a great conception," said General Dumka. "It is called Boadicea. The umbrella," he explained, "will be a trident."

"Quoi!" said the backer.

"Boadicea," said Dumka. "She was an early British Queen."

"British," said the backer. All was explained. Anything could happen now. . . .

At a table outside a fashionable café, Natasha and Arenskaya were sitting in the sunshine sipping their chocolate. The table beside them was laden with the spring flowers they had bought in the market that morning.

"How nice it is to have the whole day to ourselves," said Natasha luxuriously.

"How nice it is not to have to go to rehearsal," agreed Arenskaya.

"I wonder how it is going?" mused Natasha.

"Like 'ell," said Arenskaya. She looked at her watch. Ten to eleven. "The little Baskova will be in tears by now," she said comfortably.

"I hope so," said Natasha.

Natasha was a nice girl when you got to know her, thought Arenskaya. How to make her happy?

"Let us go and watch her weep," she suggested.

. . . "Bring on the chariot," shouted the choreographer.

Little Igor trundled on a wheelbarrow. The backer took it without a blink.

"The true chariot is not ready yet," said Dumka. "The carpenter has trouble with the square wheels. They will not go round," he explained.

"But why are they square?" asked the backer.

"It is the great conception," said Dumka, as one in view of Zion.

Boadicea mounted the wheelbarrow. She brandished

her umbrella. The piano galloped. The corps-de-ballet beat its breasts and ran round in circles. The man who was no Nijinsky came in staggering under Katusha. She was the human sacrifice. Aliosha had yet to hear of this. The man who was no Nijinsky laid her on three chairs and stabbed her with considerable satisfaction.

The music coagulated.

"Chariot off," shouted Nevajno.

But it was Boadicea who came off.

The calm choreographer clawed the air and screamed.

In the doorway, arms entwined, Natasha and Arenskaya laughed joyously together.

"Come with me to my fitting," said Natasha. "It seems we are not needed here."

"Un petit moment," said Arenskaya. She minced into the room. "In this company," she announced to the ceiling, "we do not demand much of our ballerinas, but we do prefer that they should at least stand up."

She minced back to the door. She linked arms with Natasha. They smiled joyously at the company. Arenskaya winked. They went.

"It is a plot," screamed the little Baskova at their disappearing backs. "He tilted the wheelbarrow."

The choreographer silenced her. "Back to the beginning," he said with all the dignity of an exiled monarch forecasting his early return.

His best friend sniffed.

They resumed the rehearsal. Stroganoff came heavily in. He stood watching moodily. This time the little Baskova remained on the wheelbarrow, but that was the most that could be said for her.

"Bon jour, mon ami," called the backer, tearing his fascinated gaze away from the little Baskova's precarious balance. "All is well—yes?"

"No," said Stroganoff. The time had come to speak plainly. He drew the backer over to the mantelpiece, tugged his tie three times, blew his nose, and prepared to take the plunge.

"My friend," he said, "let me put to you a hypothetical case."

"She had the night late," said the backer defensively.

"My friend, we must face the fácts," said Stroganoff. "Your little friend has the talent—but it is not for the dance."

"That is true," said the backer fairly. "But she is so pretty to look at that who will mind this?"

"Suppose," said Stroganoff, "that, for the sake of argument, I take away the lead from the little Baskova."

"Then," said the backer, "for the sake of argument, I take away my money."

"So," said Stroganoff. He sighed heavily at his entangled corps-de-ballet.

"And now," said Nicholas Nevajno blissfully, "we have the earthquake. . . ."

★   ★   ★

That afternoon Aliosha Stroganoff decided to take a hand. He had lunched with his son and Vladimir had not touched his roast goose. And when the Stroganoffs refused roast goose, or any other form of food, things were serious. So while the trained seals undulated where ballerinas would later float, he made his way to the wardrobe where the mamoushka was ironing Natasha's tu-tu to the hum of old Medinka's sewing machine.

"Old woman," he said, "I wish to talk to you." He waddled himself to a chair by the mamoushka and folded his hands across his stomach.

The mamoushka went on ironing.

"Your daughter is giving my son no peace," said Aliosha. "He is worn to a shadow."

"I had not noticed this," said the mamoushka. She turned over the tu-tu. She went on ironing.

"He is a wreck," said Aliosha. "There are rings under his eyes and he does not eat his roast goose. It was not for this," he pointed out, "that I bring him to Petersburg."

"And it is not for others to dance the lead that I bring my Natasha," said the mamoushka. She shook out the tu-tu.

"Woman, you are a fool," said Aliosha. "Where the money is—there goes the rôle. It is a law of nature." He replaced his hands across his stomach.

"Why is it not your money, old skin-the-flint?" The mamoushka turned on him. "You grudge to ruin yourself for your only son. You should be ashamed." She took the tu-tu off the board and shook it at him. Aliosha snatched it from her and threw it on the floor.

"When you are dead and buried," he said, "Vladimir will be happy."

"In the meantime, while I am still alive I take my darling to Diaghilev," retorted the mamoushka. "And if Vladimir hang himself, which," she said contemptuously, "he will never do, then it will be your fault." She stamped her foot. "Baskova must go."

"Woman, be silent," thundered Aliosha. "Baskova stays. It is signed, agreed and paid for. It can gain you nothing that my son should lead the life of a dog with a cat," he pointed out. "You have but to speak the word to your daughter and she will be as sweet as the sugar on the Easter cake for, as women go, there is not much harm in her."

"I will speak the word to my daughter," promised the mamoushka. "I will speak the word that will turn her into a wild cat. I will tell her she is too soft with your Vladimir. I will tell her to take his money, to bleed him to death, to drive him into his grave. I will tell her," she finished, "to go to Diaghilev."

Aliosha got up. His stomach heaved.

"Woman," he thundered, "I have heard enough of your nonsense. I will send for my little father. He," he threatened, "will know how to deal with you."

"And I," said the mamoushka unexpectedly, "will send for my old mamoushka."

They shook their fists at each other while old Medinka went on treadling. They would never get the curtain up if she stopped her work for little scenes like this.

★　　★　　★

The still of the night. The shutters creaked, the blinds

swung, outside the-shan't-get-home-till-mornings seemed unlikely to make it even then, but inside the darkened bedroom of the Stroganoffs all was quiet.

But not for long.

"My darling," said Stroganoff, his troubles heavy on him, "I am not happy."

The humped back of Natasha hardly moved. Very tentatively Stroganoff put an arm around it. This time the movement was definite. It was away from him.

"So," said Stroganoff. He unswung his arm, turned himself to the other side, and lay there fuming. Presently he addressed the wall.

"So," he said. "I bring her to Petersburg, I ruin the little grandfather, I am polite to the mamoushka, I owe the fortune for the flowers every time she dances, and what come of all this? The back!"

"The best years of my life," said Natasha to the other wall. "All my charm. All my talent that other managements beg me for. And what do I get? Not even the sleep in peace."

"Sleep!" Stroganoff said to his wall. "I have not closed the eye for three nights."

"It is the lie," said Natasha turning violently. "All last night you snored. Now be silent and let me sleep." She humped back again.

"I have married a witch," said Stroganoff. "A true daughter of a dancer's mother. For you I have made myself into a wreck—even the strangers in the street have pity for me. Even Arenskaya, who should be our enemy, is sorry for me."

"Arenskaya is a very sweet girl," said Natasha. "She is stupid only to bury herself in your silly company." She jerked herself away so violently that she nearly fell out of bed.

"Is it my fault that the Baskova will not do the walk out?" demanded Stroganoff. "Have we not all done our best to insult her? Me, you, Nevajno, even Katusha. Is it my fault that she burst into the tears instead of the fury?"

"The insult to that one is no use," said Natasha. "If she will not give up the rôle you must take it from her."

"But then the backer take away the money!" said Stroganoff. "Have I not told you this a million times!"

"So do not tell me again," said Natasha. "I wish to sleep." She humped.

Stroganoff closed his eyes. The image of the little Baskova floated—well, not exactly floated—before him. He opened them quickly.

The sleeping draught! He would take the sleeping draught. He would sleep like a log and snore like a wild boar and Natasha could shake him till she was tired and he would not hear her. Maybe she'd be sorry then! Or was he muddled?

The sleeping draught was in his waistcoat pocket. It meant getting out of bed. But it was worth it. Or in his trousers. Or on the shelf. One little drop, Arenskaya had said. He would take two little drops. Three. He would fall asleep at once and remain insensible for twelve hours. Lost to the world. No backer. No Baskova. No business. No performance. . . . Mon Dieu!

Inspiration hit Stroganoff. He sat up in bed. He thought

it over. He couldn't see a flaw anywhere. Foolproof! He thumped his wife's back.

"Mama," screamed Natasha waking suddenly, "now he assaults me."

"I embrace you, my darling," crowed Stroganoff. "Our troubles are over. The little Baskova does not dance. We celebrate." He hugged her.

"But what is this?" said Natasha, too overwhelmed to resist. "What good news can have come to you in the middle of the night?"

"It comes from the head," said Stroganoff. "It is my flair as an impresario that has triumphed. So, my darling, it is necessary that from now on you attend all the rehearsals as the understudy so that you know the part well."

"Me, understudy!" said Natasha. "Never!"

"It must be made to appear so," explained Stroganoff. "But you and I will know that at the first performance it is you who will be dancing."

"And the little Baskova?"

"She must suspect nothing," said Stroganoff. "It will be a pact between you and me. You must not even tell your mamoushka."

Natasha thought it over. "Vladimir," she said, "I have in you the confidence complete. But if you fail me again . . ."

"Fail you!" said Stroganoff. "Impossible . . ."

"And if anything goes wrong . . ."

Stroganoff kissed her warmly. "Then," he promised, "I give you to Diaghilev."

Natasha relaxed. She was very young and there was no

mamoushka present to sniff cold water on the promises.

"You are the dearest husband in the world," she said for the first time since the Stroganoff company had opened in the capital.

Stroganoff thought happily of his sleeping draught. No need to get out of bed to get it now.

CHAPTER XVII

To-night at 9:00 P.M.

But at the moment it was the afternoon.

The capital, if not agog, was quite interested. The publicity for the new Nevajno had worked well; all the newspapers had given space to welcoming if cautiously worded announcements of the startling experiment at the Boris Goudonov. There was also a certain amount of speculation about the new ballerina from Vladivostok, whom no critic had been permitted to view in class or at rehearsal. "A second Trefilova," they said at the Cubat—some of them.

On paper the evening was an assured success.

"Later, they pay," said Stroganoff buoyantly.

"Later, they pay," agreed the proprietor of the little restaurant round the corner. He passed a resigned pencil.

But Natasha was pensive.

"It is already two o'clock, Vladimir," she pointed out, "and the little Baskova has not even sprained an ankle."

"Relax, my little pigeon," said Stroganoff. "Have in me the confidence carefree. All goes according to plan."

His hand stole to his waistcoat pocket.

* * *

To-night at 9:00 P.M. It was 9:00 P.M.

The new Nevajno was preceded by a divertissement from Casse-Noisette.

Natasha danced the Sugar Plum. She danced it beautifully and looked like a thunder cloud.

Backstage Nevajno had dropped into the star's dressing-room for a few last words of encouragement.

"You dance bad and I kill you," he said, and strode out.

The little Baskova turned to her protector.

"Why do they all hate me?" she asked. "What have I done?"

"They are jealous of you," said the backer comfortingly. "But soon," he promised, "they will all love you."

The door kicked open. Stroganoff came in, balancing a tray of glasses with one hand and carrying a bucket in the other. In the bucket surrounded by ice reposed a bottle of champagne.

"A toast to your performance," he said. He arranged the glasses on the table.

"See," said the backer, "here is one who loves you already."

With the air of a celestial maître d'hôtel about to offer the moon, Stroganoff poured out the slightly flat champagne and passed it to the little Baskova.

"Before the performance?" asked the dancer dubiously.

"One little glass," said the maître d'hôtel. "Poof—you will dance all the better for it."

"And me?" said the backer thirstily.

"Bien sûr," said Stroganoff delighted. He poured.

"And you?" said the backer.

Stroganoff nearly dropped the bottle.

"Me—no," he said quickly. "I must keep the head cool for my speech."

"Nonsense," said the backer. "Drink, we insist."

"But it is very important, my speech," said Stroganoff. "Full of the words difficult." He groped for them. "British Constitution," he produced unexpectedly.

"Drink," urged the little Baskova. "I shan't touch a drop until you do."

Stroganoff gazed at her with the hurt reproach of a hooked mackerel betrayed by its favourite sprat. "But it is to pay you the compliment that I carry the heavy bucket up all those stairs," he protested. "Come, my little one," he entreated. "Drink to give me pleasure."

"Not until you do," said the little Baskova mutinously. At any moment she might dash her glass to the floor.

"My darling!" Stroganoff invented wildly. "I would love to drink with you. But I have—I have—the gout terrible," he began to limp, "and my doctor . . ."

"Well, anyway, I'm going to drink," declared the backer. He tossed off his glass.

What use was that, thought Stroganoff crossly.

"If you don't drink," said the little Baskova with a distinct edge in her voice, "I do not go on."

A gleam of hope lit Stroganoff's face only to flicker out again as a thin spatter of applause came floating through the corridor to act as a spur to the little Baskova's ambition.

"Mon Dieu—my make-up!" she said, and fled to her dressing-table.

The applause died away. Casse-Noisette was over. In fifteen minutes Boadicea would be on.

The backer stretched himself. "Aie!" he said, "but I am sleepy." He poured himself a second glass. He poured out for Stroganoff. "Drink," he invited.

Impossible to delay any longer. Stroganoff clutched his glass, chinked with the little Baskova's, raised it and waited. He realized that she was waiting for him. No escape! The things that I do for my darling, he thought.

"God bless us all," he said manfully and drank.

"Amen to that," said the backer. He could hardly keep his eyes open.

"God bless you both," said the little Baskova. She gulped joyously.

The door opened. In it stood Natasha, a pale pink foam of frozen sugar.

"Ah—the little wife," said the backer just managing to recognize her. "Come drink to our success, my darling." He lurched towards the bottle.

"Non!" cried Stroganoff. "Non!" He swayed. "Not before the performance."

"Drink to my success," said the little Baskova. She yawned.

Resolution came to Natasha. "Yes," she hissed, "I will drink. I will drink to," she raised her glass, "Diaghilev."

"Non!" cried Stroganoff. "Non! Non! British Conshti-shonshon."

"To Diaghilev," toasted Natasha. She drank.

★　　★　　★

Five minutes later Arenskaya peeped in.

Well, well, well, she thought. What was it that Kash-kavar Jones always said about the linings of the English clouds?

She set about taking off the sleeping Baskova's costume.

*　　*　　*

The Cubat restaurant was thronged.

Here, that part of the world of fashion which had not gone to the Boris Goudonov was waiting to meet that segment which had. You could hardly see the trelliswork for roses, and you could not speak for the popping of champagne corks. If you did catch a word it sounded like "Baskova."

For everybody who had not been to the Boris Goudonov was waiting anxiously for anybody who had. The new divine dancer from Vladivostok whom nobody had been permitted to glimpse until to-night—was she divine? Not a ballerina in the room who did not cross herself when she thought of her. The rumours were encouraging, but you could never trust a rumour. She might be good after all.

In the centre of the room a table had been laid for twenty-seven covers. It had been ordered by Vladimir Stroganoff to celebrate the triumph of the Nevajno ballet. Twenty-six of them were empty. At the twenty-seventh sat the choreographer stolidly celebrating. With an impossible-to-awaken host the other guests had tactfully omitted to turn up, but the choreographer did not appear to notice his absence. He ate and he drank and he appeared to be quite happy. From time to time he drew on the tablecloth.

The other tables took him for the first arrival, but as the minutes went by and Nevajno went on eating and drinking and drawing, speculation ran wild.

What had happened at the Boris Goudonov?

The clientele looked reproachfully at Almire Cubat. What was he there for if not to gather gossip for them?

Kshessinskaya pointed imperiously. So did Pavlova and Preobrajenska. Cubat looked towards the preoccupied choreographer. With the cautious air of an ambassador about to scrutinize a peace treaty he negotiated the distance.

"How did the evening go?" he asked. "A triumph, I trust."

The choreographer looked up. "Cabbages," he said curtly.

"Cabbages?"

"They threw them," said Nevajno. He went on eating. Cubat negotiated his way back.

"Cabbages," he told Kshessinskaya, Preobrajenska and Pavlova.

"But the little Baskova!" clamoured Pavlova, Preobrajenska and Kshessinskaya. "What was she like?"

Cubat spread his hands.

But they had stopped looking at him, anyway. For on the staircase stood a radiant figure, her arms full of flowers and her eyes sparkling with delight. It was Arenskaya.

It was seen at once that she was wearing Natasha's ermine cloak.

With her was General Dumka. He was carrying an enormous basket of orchids. You could not tell that this was meant for the little Baskova until you looked at the writing on the ribbon.

Cubat bowed. "The others will be here soon?" he asked.

"Mais non," said Arenskaya.

She allowed Cubat to lead her to the table, bowing left and right and blowing kisses, and seated, entered immediately into animated conversation, unanswered by the abstracted Dumka on one side and the drawing choreographer on the other.

"The evening was a success?" ventured Cubat.

"For me, yes," said Arenskaya. "Ah, Almire, you should have been there. I dance as I never dance before. The shouting!" She glowed.

Almire bowed low and drifted off. He ignored the uplifted fingers at the other tables. The most sophisticated restaurateur in the world was not going to ask a ballerina to talk of the performance of another while she was talking about her own. The evening lay ahead. Ah—here was M'sieur Svetlov.

But Svetlov was in a hurry. "Appalling, appalling!" he muttered and started to scribble. At his elbow his runner stood waiting and practically peering over his shoulder.

"He gives me hell," said Nevajno, as one who welcomed it. "One sees it in his eye."

"Yes, yes?" said Arenskaya. "But what he give me?"

A handsome guardsman came in. He bent over Arenskaya and kissed her hand. "My princess," he said, "you were divine." He walked away. He was engulfed.

All over the restaurant the news bubbled up between champagne corks.

Arenskaya had danced Boadicea! Arenskaya!

What a relief!

Kshessinskaya, Pavlova and Preobrajenska relaxed.

Karsavina and Kyasht could breathe again.

Trefilova came rushing into the room. She bowed quickly to Cubat. She did not wait for the orchestra to burst into Lac des Cygnes. She hardly paused to exhibit her new bracelet. She rushed over to Svetlov.

"Valerien," she said, "tell me, sans blague, is she a second Trefilova?"

"Tranquillize yourself, my dear," said Svetlov. "She is a little girl who has drunk too much champagne and fallen asleep in her dressing-room."

"Before or after?" breathed Trefilova.

"All through," snarled Svetlov. He ran his pencil viciously over the page.

Down the marble steps, supported on two sticks, his head shaking with ague, his buttonhole sporting a carnation, hobbled a general. Who said he was past it all? Now that his wife was dead at last he was going out again. Every night of his life. Seventeen years since a ballerina had called him Bobka. Soon put that right. . . . Confound that bottom stair!

He crabbed his way across the room and came to a shaky halt beside Arenskaya. He quivered her little hand up to his lips.

"Divine, Baskova," he trebled. "Mademoiselle, you have made me very happy to-night."

Dumka giggled. "It is Arenskaya," he said.

But happily the General had died.

CHAPTER XVIII

A_{ND SO}," Stroganoff told the sandy man, "you will understand, my friend, that for the next few nights I sleep alone."

The sandy man nodded.

"Only," said Stroganoff, "I do not sleep."

"What about the sleeping draught?" asked the sandy man.

"No more of that," said Stroganoff. "The headache with which I awake in the little Baskova's dressing-room. Aie!" He clasped his head expressively. "I can think of nothing; my plan exploded—what has become of my first night? My Natasha—what she will do to our marriage? Or what the mamoushka who has awaken us is saying? All that I think of is the aspirin. And as for the others, they, too, think only of their heads. But later, when they are recovered, it is different."

"I can imagine it," said the sandy man.

"You cannot imagine it," said Stroganoff firmly. "It takes a Russian impresario with the plan exploded to imagine it. But, in short, my friend, at once everything is the ka-put."

The sunlight was bright and spiteful. It flooded the room and meanly lit up an unshaven Stroganoff in his dressing-gown, slumped on his bed.

He had a headache. It was not the same headache but a new and worse one. It had been brought on by listening to a succession of people telling him what they thought of him at the top of their voices.

The little Baskova had screamed off the accumulation of her humiliations since her arrival in the capital. The backer had encouraged her, for, if she stopped screaming at Stroganoff, she would start screaming at him. When she had reduced herself to hysterics in a corner, the backer had taken over and removed his backing in a bellow. Hard on the slammed door that signified their departure came the mamoushka, and though she was not so loud, she was twice as shrill. No, he could not see Natasha. He would never see her again.

Natasha came in to confirm this. They wept together, they consoled each other, they pointed out that they had each other left—Natasha and the mamoushka that is. They swore they were going straight to Diaghilev. They swiped Stroganoff's bottle of aspirins and were on their way.

Then Aliosha had come in heaving with indignation.

"My Katusha!" he boomed. "A sacrifice to a plot that not even a schoolboy would stoop to attempt. I find the backer—all right, you find him—who find him make no difference. Now he has gone. And we are left with the bills, and unless I am to pay them myself, which God forbid, I have to appeal to the little grandfather, and what you think he will say to me?"

"What you are saying to me," said Stroganoff. He groaned.

"I am too soft," Aliosha reproached himself. "That is what is the matter with me. If I had any sense I would close your theatre and take you back to Omsk. And if Natasha leaves you that is your business."

"She has left me already," said Stroganoff.

"A nice state of affairs," said Aliosha indignantly. "My son is twenty-seven and he does not yet know how to hold a woman. It seems that I have to teach you that, too." He melted a little. "I will talk with her," he promised.

"She is with the mamoushka," said Stroganoff.

"H'm," said Aliosha. "I will talk with her later."

He waddled out.

Stroganoff pondered his woes as deeply as the continually ringing telephone would allow. No money. No credit. Nobody trusted him any more. Even the proprietor of the little restaurant round the corner had rung up to plead that he was only a poor tradesman.

Nicholas Nevajno came in. He enquired after Stroganoff's head, improved it, and dismissed it.

"Your head is better? Yes. Good. Have you seen the notices?"

Notices! It showed the state he was in that he had not yet given a thought to the papers. The unquenchable optimism that was the soul of Stroganoff soared up. His ballet was a sensation! The day was saved!

"Show me," he demanded.

The ballet was a sensation. The day was not saved.

"It is as I expected," said Nevajno, not at all displeased.

"I am in advance of my time." The word "advance" reminded him of something. He asked for it.

"Go away," said Stroganoff. "If I give you a scheque now it will be like one of yours."

"Like mine?" Nevajno rubbed his chin. Depressed, he wandered out.

No marriage. No money. No credit. Back to Omsk.

A bright little head peered round the door.

"Vladimir," cooed Arenskaya. "Here I am. You bless me—no?"

"Me!" said Stroganoff. He looked at the donor of the sleeping draught.

Arenskaya, who had worked out that this must be the perfect moment to ask for a rise, came prancing in and put her arms gently round Vladimir's unshaven neck.

"I am so happy, Vladimir," she cooed. "So happy to have saved the day for you."

"Did you strangle her?" asked the sandy man. "No," he remembered.

"No," agreed Stroganoff. "But before she go she is another person who tell me what she think of me."

"But at least Diaghilev didn't drop in," said the sandy man consolingly.

"No," said Stroganoff brightening. "For that one had his troubles, too. . . ."

"Sergei," said Karsavina. "Stop shilly-shallying. I tell you I have to know. I tell you I must tell Teleyakov whether I go with you by noon to-day and I cannot put it off till after to-morrow morning at latest. Yes, Sergei, I have the patience, but also I am not the fool. I tell you I must know . . . Sergei . . . Exchange, have you cut me off?"

Or had he hung up? She wondered.

Diaghilev had hung up.

"Women," he said scornfully. "All they can think of is their own affairs. Now I will have to take her sweetmeats and talk for three hours and not commit myself and be charming all the time." He scowled.

A cry of slightly acid mourning arose from the cortège.

"Teleyakov ought to be sacked," said Benois.

"Teleyakov ought to be shot," said Bakst.

"Teleyakov is an ass," said Diaghilev.

For Teleyakov had been working upon the Government to withdraw their backing for Diaghilev's European tour. To-day the news had come through that he had succeeded. If the tour was to take place at all it must do so from private funds and with artists willing to face the displeasure of the State theatres. And, with little Ginsberg stretched to his maximum, the prospects of Diaghilev's getting to Paris seemed about as bright as those of the man from Omsk. And Tatia telephoning every two minutes for her contract. What did that one want with a contract, anyway? Didn't she trust him to pay her? Sometime.

"Ah, if one could only work with men always," said Diaghilev. "A man can see the whole canvas and not be bounded by his own part of it."

"True," said Benois judicially. "Very true. Aie me," he sighed, "that my sets for Petroushka will not be seen in Paris!"

"Paris!" said Stravinsky. "What stimulation can a musician get in Petersburg. Grand Dukes!" He spat.

"What use to show a Russian fair to Russian people!" said Fokine. "They know it," he pointed out.

"In Paris," mourned Nijinsky, "they would give me all the ballet shoes I need."

"Silence," thundered Diaghilev. "I will take you to Paris. Have I not said so? All that I ask is to be left in peace to find out how. Or rather," he decided, "I will leave you." He strode to the door. "With your permission," he remembered.

"Something is worrying Sergei," said P. Puthyk as the door closed, if not with a slam at least sharply.

*   *   *

Early summer had descended on St. Petersburg in a shower of sunshades. Sunshades sprouted from Victorias, sunshades burgeoned from the pavements, sunshades bloomed from terraces and café tables. Even if you had come out without your sunshade, you could hardly avoid sitting under someone else's. The sky was blue and the snows had melted and if the church bells weren't ringing in the middle of the afternoon you knew, that they would start at any moment.

Sergei Diaghilev, on his way to reason with the director of the State Theatres, had decided to walk. Already he was regretting this. From the outset the arguments he had hoped to assemble had been interrupted by a series of beckoning sunshades. All had to be bowed to, some had to be chatted to, and nobody must be told anything.

"Sergei!" A formidable aged Princess, who had known him since he was so high—always a disadvantage—beckoned imperiously to her crested landau. "What is this nonsense I hear, Sergei?"

"It is nonsense," said Diaghilev smoothly. He kissed her hand.

"Now don't lie to me," said the Princess. "I have known you since you were so high," she reminded him.

"Highness, I am taller now," said Diaghilev. He bowed and walked on.

Satisfying, he reflected, but tactless. On the other hand, he cheered himself up, the Princess had never paid for a seat yet. Ah, well!

Outside a fashionable café, St. Petersburg was refreshing itself. Diaghilev bowed to a strawberry ice but looked quickly away from a chocolate angel cake.

A parasol detached itself from an animated group and floated diffidently but definitely towards him. Behind it, like a swollen echo, wafted a slightly larger parasol, less diffident but more definite.

Mon Dieu, thought Diaghilev, she has also a mother! "Enchanté," he bowed as Natasha presented her.

"M'sieur Diaghilev," the charming smile of the mamoushka would have deceived anyone but an impresario, "our contract has not yet arrived."

"Tiens, you astonish me," said Diaghilev, who had not yet drawn it up. "You shall get it to-morrow," he promised.

"For Paris?" pursued the mamoushka.

So she had heard too—the hag!

"And six curtains?" asked Natasha.

"Everything is possible," said Diaghilev.

He passed on. He crossed the public gardens, threading his way through the crested carriages. Now all was green and calm with only the shouts of the children to remind him how quiet it was here.

Diaghilev stood and gazed at the swans floating decoratively about the lake.

And not a ballerina among them!

Diaghilev wished he were a farmer. He decided he didn't really. The difficult but rewarding life of the successful impresario, bringing miracles to reality by a commission here, a suggestion there, and a lightning rehearsal lasting twenty-four hours; assembling the groping genius of others into the forcing frame of fashion, filling his theatres with the grace of his dancers and ringing up on them by the grace of God, travelling from capital to capital till the very whisper of Diaghilev stood for excitement and colour and the avant garde—that was the only life for him. But he had to have money to lead it. How much did he owe? What did that matter! How much could he owe? That was important.

He gazed at a drake whose beady eye reminded him of his bank manager.

"Maestro, you waste your time," said a voice at his elbow. "All that can be done with swans has been done already—by Petipa."

Diaghilev turned. It was the choreographer who did the impossible ballets for the provincial from Omsk.

"Young man, you are wrong," said Diaghilev. "There is much to be done with a swan yet. Fokine has a conception but he insists that it needs Pavlova to dance it. And Pavlova will not come to me, though I beg and beg her." He frowned. "It is her one mistake."

"Pavlova—poof!" said Nicholas Nevajno.

"That, too, is a point of view," agreed Diaghilev. He gazed into the green secrets of the lake. Money . . . money . . . money . . . he was thinking.

"Excuse me," said Nevajno, "but to-day it happen that by great chance I am out without any money. So," he suggested confidently, "you schange me schmall scheque."

Diaghilev looked at him. He began to roar with laughter.

*　　*　　*

In the director's office at the Maryinsky, Teleyakov looked at the visiting card that his secretary had handed to him.

"Diaghilev," he said. "Well, well, well. Keep him waiting for ten minutes."

He opened a newspaper.

*　　*　　*

"And how is little Ginsberg?" asked Teleyakov politely. "Flourishing, I trust?"

He was enjoying himself. Diaghilev was here to ask for favours. Diaghilev, who for years had treated him with polite contempt. Diaghilev, who had never sought his opinions and only listened to them because he had to. Diaghilev, who deflowered his theatres of his best dancers. Diaghilev, who produced new-fangled nonsense and discordant music out of the air and sold them to the capital as the last word in art. Diaghilev, who always referred to him as a last-ditch-donkey. Diaghilev was here to ask for favours. And he wasn't going to get them.

"Flourishing, I hope?" he repeated.

Diaghilev did not move a muscle. He was not enjoying himself. To beg for favours from this man, whose life began and ended with Petipa—it almost made you a reactionary.

"Ginsberg is well enough," he said smoothly. Oppressed moujiks! What about oppressed impresarios? "Let us come to the point," he suggested.

"By all means," purred Teleyakov. "Anything I can do." Come, my little Sergei, he was thinking. Plead!

Damned if I'm going to, thought Diaghilev.

"You know why I am here," he said. "You have done me great harm. Me, Europe and Russia. I would advise you to undo it while you can."

War! Teleyakov almost rubbed his hands.

"My friend," he said, "why should the State Theatre lend you its money, its best dancers, its prestige? In what way does it benefit Russia to have a lot of pretentious nonsense shown abroad? One day," he looked through the wall, "I will persuade the Tzar to let me take the State Theatre abroad and show Europe the true Russian tradition as it has been danced in this establishment for hundreds of years."

"My friend," said Diaghilev, and was he gritting his teeth? "I am not in the mood nor have I the time to argue artistic matters with you now. We have fought over this ground many times in the past—we shall never agree. I am here to ask you to restore the Government backing that you have taken from me," he said bluntly.

"Why should I?" said Teleyakov, suddenly coming out into the open. "Why should I work for a project of which I do not approve?"

"Because Europe approves. Listen, my friend," Diaghilev leant forward, "I only need your dancers for the summer season when the State Theatre is closed and the dancers are resting or on loan to the provinces. Help me in this and it cannot harm you. It may even," he paused meaningly, "benefit you substantially."

The little bribe! Teleyakov had been waiting for it. It only needed this to make his happiness complete. He chose to ignore the implication.

"Why should I?" he repeated. "Why should I foster a project which gives me a lot of trouble and against which my artistic conscience cries out. Why," it burst from him, "should I use my influence to add to your transient glory?"

"Transient!" Diaghilev's deadly politeness disappeared. He rose awfully to his feet. "Let me tell you, my little Government official, that the only reason posterity will hear about you is because of the books they will read about me. So," he demanded with his hands spread flat on the desk, "do I get my backing, or don't I?"

"Damned if you do," said Teleyakov. He thumped the desk.

"That is how the great ones in Russia talk the business." Stroganoff sighed to the sandy man. "Always the politeness, always the manner," he put his hand on his heart, "correct. Not like in your Europe where you shout and you scream and you thump the desk."

The sandy man smiled. "So it was the bottoms for Diaghilev," he said.

"For the moment—yes," agreed Stroganoff. "But if it was the bottoms for Diaghilev," he shrugged, "it was not yet the tops for me."

★　　★　　★

Thunder in the air. All day long the company had been listless. Only the hardiest dancers had turned up to class, and, as there was no new work being rehearsed, the men had spent the afternoon playing Vint and No Nijinsky had gambled his overcoat away. It was several sizes too small for Little Igor, but at least he could always gamble it back again.

The girls passed the time darning their ballet shoes and washing each other's hair and trying not to spend money for they had been on half wages for weeks. Natasha and Arenskaya went driving in the Park. But not together. Now that the little Baskova had gone there was no longer any reason for it.

Stroganoff had spent the day doing his accounts, but even that optimistic adder-up could not tot them into profit. The only surplus was vegetables. St. Petersburg had taken to dropping into the upper reaches of the Boris Goudonov (25 kopecs) and throwing them at Boadicea.

"But we lose less money this week than last," said Stroganoff, closing the ledger with a defiant bang.

"But we still lose," said Dumka depressed.

Now it was evening and the company was projecting listless Swans on a lackadaisical lake to a half-filled house.

In the wings a flowing moustache was expressing its views to a bald-headed dome. The circus proprietor had tracked down Stroganoff.

"My friend," he was saying, "let us talk frankly. Your ballet is not stimulating my business. In fact, it is doing me harm."

Stroganoff gazed at the stage. "Mon Dieu!" he said as the Swan Queen swooned into No Nijinsky's arms—luckily there.

"Before you came," said the circus proprietor, "I was playing every night to capacity—well almost," he admitted. "And now my houses are but little better than yours."

Stroganoff drew himself up. "And is this my fault?" he demanded, a truculent camel refusing to break its back with someone else's last straw.

"I am a man of honour," said the proprietor. "I pay my wages, I feed my animals well, and I honour the note of hand of my little grandfather. But," he pointed out, "it would have been cheaper for me to have done this with money."

"Money," said Stroganoff bitterly.

"My friend," said the proprietor, "I have to live. And I cannot do this while the public comes here to see my circus and finds instead—this," he waved his arm in the direction of a huddle of huntsmen, "and so does not come again."

"And what of me?" asked Stroganoff hotly. "The balleto-mane come here to be whisked to dreams of an enchanted land," he waved his arms towards a wobbly pas-de-bourrée, "and when they come on the wrong night they find instead—this." He pointed to the wedged-in-the-corner elephant.

"My friend," said the proprietor. "There is one public for the circus and one for the ballet, and sooner than confuse themselves they both stay away. No, no, my friend, one of us must go."

Stroganoff brightened. "When you leave?" he demanded.

Aliosha came wandering up, a sheaf of bills in his hands.

"Vladimir," he announced. "I have decided. On Sunday I go back to Omsk."

"I shall miss you, papoushka," said Stroganoff relieved.

"You will not miss me," said papoushka. "You will be with me."

"Ah," said the circus proprietor.

"But, papoushka!" The camel sagged. "My career! My Natasha's career. Your Katusha's career," he appealed desperately.

"It is no use," said Aliosha. "I and the little father have given you your wish. But if we continue we will soon begin to lose our own money."

"Meanwhile you lose mine," said the circus proprietor.

"Is it our fault that your little grandfather ran into debt?" said Aliosha coldly. He turned his back.

The proprietor wandered over and patted the elephant. Would he have to pledge him? Never!

"You are not fair, papoushka," said Stroganoff. "In Petersburg success does not come at once. Already I have moved many mountains. Would you take me away while I am pushing at others?"

Aliosha looked the other way. "Your orchestra is terrible," he said.

"We are losing money, it is true," argued Stroganoff. "But each week we lose less and less. Now I am nearly established. When I go to the Cubat the proprietor bows. I walk in the gardens and I say 'Hallo' all the time. Do not," he appealed, "dash from me the vodka before it flow down my throat."

"Anyone can lose money," said Aliosha, a chip off the old block, "but it takes a wise man to know when to stop. My son—you are not a success in the capital. It is not your fault," he conceded. "The competition is too strong for you. Give in and come home."

"Little father," said Stroganoff, "I am your son. Did you give in when you had the fire before you were ensured?"

"No," said Aliosha. "But," he pointed out, "it was my own money that I was losing."

"And me, I will not lose yours," promised Stroganoff. "All that I need now is the little coup. One success and Petersburg is at my feet. If I could get a Pavlova. Just one Pavlova," he emphasized.

Aliosha was silent.

"Papoushka," pleaded Stroganoff, "write to the little grandfather."

Aliosha fumbled inside his pockets. "It is not necessary," he confessed. "He will be here to-morrow." He pulled out a wire and passed it to his son. It read:

Decided to look into things myself. Arriving by train to-morrow. Father.

"Voilà!" said Aliosha. He looked a little scared himself.

*   *   *

Conseille de famille.

The Stroganoffs were seated round the table in Aliosha's bed-sitting-room. Hope in adversity had united the family and a photographer, happening to press a bulb at this moment, would have caught Vladimir smiling at his mother-in-law and the daughter smiling at her husband. Also present was General Dumka smiling on all of them.

"We must give the little grandfather the welcome tremendous," Stroganoff was saying. "It must be quite clear that it is for himself alone that we hug and kiss him. You, papoushka," he divided the labours, "shall engage for him the room silent on the south side. You, Natasha, shall select the books that he will not read in it—but they must be there. You, mamoushka, will have ready for him the collation delicious, and I," he took on the hardest labour, "shall go down to the station and listen to how he did not like the journey."

"And me?" said Dumka, left out of it. "What do I do?"

Stroganoff pondered. "You," he decided, "shall push the bath-chair and you must remember to take the corners slowly and also," memory travelled back, "never to leave him in it on top of a hill."

"Aie!" said Aliosha. "What a day that was."

"It is our one chance," said Stroganoff. "We must make the old one so happy that he will not remember to ask for our figures. We must forget our quarrels, we must forget Diaghilev, we must all love one another." He looked at Natasha.

"That is right," said the mamoushka. (No contract from Diaghilev yet.) "That is right, my little one," she said encouragingly.

Natasha coloured.

"And that night," Stroganoff told the sandy man, "Natasha return to my room. And though it is not quite as before it was, enfin, pas mal. Pas mal du tout," he remembered.

CHAPTER XIX

T
HE great terminus of St.
Petersburg was a forcing frame of joined-together black
beetles. They chuffed, they shunted, and they let off steam,
while all around them on the platforms an army of ants
wept, embraced and presented roast chickens.

A bell rang three times. A beetle chuffed bravely out to
a trail of waving handkerchiefs, "go with Gods," "love to
Aunt Katyas," and "don't lean out of the windows."

"I wonder why I wanted to be an engine-driver," mused
the engine-driver. The stoker went on stoking.

Through the home-going ants and the cries of "you forgot to give her the water melon," two ants were progressing
arm in arm. One had white whiskers, the other a bald dome.
Between them they carried a huge box of chocolates from
which they absently refreshed themselves from time to
time.

"See, my friend," said Stroganoff triumphantly. "Did I
not tell you we would not be late?"

"We would have been late had the train been early," said
Dumka stubbornly. "And then your little grandfather would
never have forgiven you and the day would have been lost.
No, no, my friend," he insisted, "it was not the moment to

linger in front of the mirror."

Stroganoff tugged at the effulgent silk on his bosom. "I am not happy about my colour scheme," he fretted. But Dumka was looking at the indicator.

"Tiens," he said in awe, "the train from Vienna is only four hours late."

"What do I care about trains from Vienna," said Stroganoff impatiently. "It is the train from Omsk that is important. Come!" He took a chocolate and forged ahead.

With the Trans-Siberian Express about to arrive two days late and the Vienna Express about to arrive four hours late, the platform was crowded. Stroganoff threaded Dumka to a point of vantage.

"Voilà," he said. "From here we will see the little grandfather leaning out of the window and greet him before he can greet us."

"The old one will be too tired to look out of the window," dampened Dumka.

"We Stroganoffs do not tire easily," boasted Vladimir. "And when the little grandfather sees what I have brought him," he held up the box of chocolates and, as an afterthought, helped himself, "and hears that instead of a droshky he will ride to the hotel in a snow-white landau with the rubber wheels—the years will drop from him and also," he dug Dumka in the ribs, "his money."

"So," said Dumka. He munched. "Next time," he announced, "I pick one with the soft centre." He explored the box.

The ants stirred like a forest in the wind. A beetle chugged triumphantly in.

"The Vienna Express," said Dumka.

"Why you worry me with Vienna," said Stroganoff. He bit into a chocolate and stared down the platform into the empty distance. "Hard," he said disappointed.

But Dumka was looking at a cluster of bouquets gathered in front of a carriage held out in worship to a small dark woman who was descending from it.

"Ciel!" he cried. "It is the divine Dourakova."

"Dourakova!" Stroganoff swung round. "But she is in Vienna," he objected.

"She has come back," breathed Dumka, gazing in worship at a mass of luggage that was piling up and rapidly hiding the ballerina.

A signal fell, but Stroganoff failed to notice. He, too, was gazing at what could still be seen of the sables that dripped from the divine Dourakova. And then he was galvanized.

"My friend," he cried. "We are mad. For what we wait? Come—we approach ourselves."

He dashed down the platform.

"Marya!" screamed Dourakova to her maid. "Hold tight to the jewel case."

"You are holding it yourself," screamed back Marya.

"And count the luggage again," instructed Dourakova, but not trusting her counted herself. "Only thirty-four pieces," she totted up. "This cannot be right," she smiled absently at General Dumka.

Stroganoff caught the recapitulating hand, guided it between a dressing-case and a hat-box and kissed a diamond ring.

"Madame," he said, "this is a great day for me."

A gaunt figure alighted from the carriage and towered over the group.

"I have a headache," it announced starkly.

"Oh, mon Dieu!" said Dourakova aghast. "My poor Grisha. We must do something. Do something!" she implored Stroganoff.

Stroganoff extended the chocolates. The gaunt figure munched.

"Soft," it said disgusted. It spat.

"Say nothing," hissed Dumka to the about-to-bridle Stroganoff. "It is Grisha Podushkin."

"I do not care if it is Rasputin," said Stroganoff. "He spit."

"But he is the leader of the claque," urged Dumka. "He organize everything."

"He does not organize this," said Stroganoff. He bowed deeply to Dourakova.

"Madame," he said, "my carriage awaits you. You get in it quick before Diaghilev he pop up. It has rubber wheels," he clinched the matter.

Dourakova hesitated.

"Come," said Stroganoff.

He picked up three valises and swept the ballerina off the platform.

From a window of the Trans-Siberian Express a beady-eyed old man from Omsk glared after him.

*　　*　　*

"M'sieur," said Dourakova, as the snow-white landau pulled up outside the Hotel Splendide and a swarm of pageboys surrounded the carriage, "it has been most kind of you to escort me to my hotel. And now I will say 'au revoir.' "

"Au revoir," agreed Stroganoff. He followed her in.

The hotel clerk bowed deeply. "Madame, the suite is ready." He stepped into the lift. So did Stroganoff.

"Voilà," said the clerk. "The first suite."

"It faces south?" asked Dourakova.

"But all the way," said the clerk.

"It is silent until noon?" pursued Dourakova. "And at the hour of the siesta?"

"As the tomb," swore the clerk.

"Is the mattress soft?"

"As a snowdrift."

"Bon," said Dourakova. "Then it will do for Grisha. You see," she confided to the clerk, "on the morning of a performance I am up at ten, but my cheer-leader must sleep until lunch. It is so exhausting for his nerves."

Stroganoff nodded profoundly. "Parfaitement," he said.

Dourakova realized him with slight surprise. "M'sieur," she said, "it is very kind of you to escort me to my rooms. But now," she held out her hand, "I will say 'au revoir.' "

Stroganoff kissed it. "Au revoir," he agreed. He stayed where he was.

The clerk led them down the corridor and opened a door.

"The second suite," he announced.

"Is there a house telephone?" asked Dourakova. "Is there a communicating door?"

"Is the water in the bathroom hot?" asked Stroganoff.

Dourakova realized him again.

"M'sieur," she insisted. "Au revoir."

"Au revoir," said Stroganoff.

"I will send up the luggage," said the clerk. He bowed himself out.

Dourakova turned to the dressing-table. She took out her hatpins, she puffed up her hair, she allowed her sables to drop from her shoulders. These long journeys were killing her. . . .

"And now," said Stroganoff, bobbing up in the mirror, "for the chat cosy."

"The gentle firmness," Stroganoff told the sandy man, "and not to take hard the snub, always the cheerful, always the hopeful—that is the way to manage the ballerina. Three times she tell me 'au revoir,' and me, I am still there." He glowed.

"And what happened then?" asked the sandy man.

"Oh, she kick me out," said Stroganoff. "But the ground is prepared, and I send round Dumka."

★   ★   ★

General Dumka stood in front of the mirror and twiddled his carnation.

"What is the time?" he asked.

"Time you went," said Vladimir Stroganoff. He kissed him on both cheeks. "And remember our destiny lies in your hands."

"Go with God," said Aliosha.

"Or we all go back to Omsk," said the little grandfather. He dug his chin in the air.

Vladimir crossed to him.

"Little grandfather," he pleaded, "why are you still angry? Have I not explained to you many times the full reasons why I do not stay to meet you at the station. Why then do you still scowl at your grandson who loves you?"

"And why should I not scowl?" demanded Moysha. "Did not the droshky try to overcharge me—*me*—an old man, who has not been to the capital for forty years but who still remembers how much one should pay a droshky?"

"Little grandfather," pleaded Vladimir. "Give Dumka your blessing. It needs only for him to bring Dourakova to us and all our troubles will be over."

"That's right," said Aliosha encouragingly. "All our troubles will be over."

"Fool," squealed Moysha. "What gives you such confidence in this dancer?"

"She is Dourakova," said Dumka reprovingly.

"The divine Dourakova," said Aliosha.

"Then pay her with your own roubles," snapped the little grandfather, "or hold your tongue."

Aliosha held his tongue.

"Dumka," said Vladimir, patting the General on the shoulder. "My brave Dumka. Be of good courage and do not forget to tell Dourakova what I have told you to say."

"I know well what to say to Dourakova," said Dumka testily. "I who have known her since she was a second soloist. Never," he sighed, "shall I forget her début in La Belle au Bois Dormant at the Maryinsky. The Breadcrumb!" he breathed ecstatically.

"Do not remind her of it," urged Vladimir. "Paint instead

the picture glowing of our company and offer her the contract fabulous."

"Eh?" said Moysha.

"Tell her," said Vladimir, "that here she will be the Assoluta of Assolutas."

Natasha came in.

"I go now," said Dumka. He picked up his cane and ran.

"He, he," chuckled Moysha. "You forgot to bless him." He waggled a finger at the transfixed Natasha. Old as he was he could recognize a situation when he saw one.

"Who?" asked Natasha ominously. "Who is to be the Assoluta of Assolutas?"

"My child!" The tactful Aliosha heaved himself out of the chair and waddled over to wrap his arms around her. "I have for you the surprise that will gladden your heart. Guess who comes to save the day? Guess whom we invite to join our company? Guess?"

"Guess, my darling." Vladimir hovered anxiously.

"The divine Dourakova," said Moysha. He had tired of the build-up.

"So," said Natasha. She wrenched herself out of Aliosha's arms.

"I see you are pleased," said Aliosha gazing at the stony face.

"Say you are pleased, my darling," pleaded Vladimir.

"Pleased!" said Natasha. She took a deep breath. "Pleased —when the Stroganoffs conspire behind my back—all three of them—to bring to my company a ballerina that shall rob me of my rôles." She glared at them. "If she comes, I go."

"It is that or Omsk," thundered Aliosha. If tact wouldn't work, he'd show her.

"Not for me," declared Natasha. "For me—Europe. For me—Diaghilev."

"Hoity-toity," said the little grandfather.

"My darling," said Vladimir. "See the reason. With Dourakova we can continue in the capital. Without her we go back to Omsk. Help me, my little wife."

But Natasha did not soften. "I must think of my career," she said.

"You should think of your husband," thundered Aliosha.

"Quite right, my son," said Moysha. "So she should."

Natasha tapped her toe. "If she comes," she said, "I go." She turned on her husband. "Well, Vladimir?"

Vladimir looked round. He saw the heaving stomach of his father, he saw the shocked expression of his little grandfather. He drew comfort from the clan.

"If she comes," he said, "you may go."

Natasha looked at him dazed.

"And that night," Stroganoff told the sandy man, "I sleep alone again. Only this time," he mused, "somehow I sleep."

★   ★   ★

A quiet night at the Cubat. The table near the service doors was empty. Almire was most upset about this. The beginning of the ruin.

But even as he put a Reserved card on it the divine Dourakova came sweeping in. Straight away there was a fresh complication. How to offer so small a table to so great a ballerina. He would have to expand.

But the divine Dourakova did not even pout. Instead she smiled at him with all the radiance of a dancer returning from a continental tour, intent on giving the impression that it has been triumphant.

"She is with little Dumka," noted Bakst, Bolm, and Benois. "Oho!" they said.

"What do I care," said Diaghilev, gazing gloomily at a sketch Nijinsky had scribbled on the tablecloth.

"Teleyakov," said Nijinsky helpfully. "I hang him." He added a loop.

At the table by the service doors the gay chatter that had started the meal fizzled out.

"So it has been a great success Vienna?" said General Dumka. "Ah, me, that I was not there!"

"A great success," said Dourakova thoughtfully. "Yes, it was a great success. But," she switched on the smile behind which she need not listen, "let us talk about you."

But General Dumka was much too wise for any such thing.

"Oh, no," he said. "I have been supping ballerinas for many years, and when one of them comes back from Vienna it is not about the old General they wish to talk." He poured out the champagne. "Come," he urged, "tell Dumka your troubles. And do not tell me you have no troubles," he said, "for I will believe anything but this."

Dourakova smiled at him—a real smile. "Dear Dumka," she said. "My troubles are not for you."

"And since when?" said Dumka indignantly. "Did I not nurse you through your first Lac des Cygnes? Did I not support you through your first Giselle? Was it not Dumka who stood by your side when you walked out of the Maryinsky?"

"You should have pushed me back," said Dourakova. "You should have pushed me back."

"I tried," said Dumka. "Don't you remember, my darling. All night I push." He mopped his brow.

Dourakova made a great confession. "I was very silly," she said. "And I was very silly, too, to make an enemy of Diaghilev." She looked across to his table. "In fact," she faced it, "I have been a fool."

"Hush," said Dumka horrified.

"It is all right," said Dourakova. "The little table quiet has its compensations. There is no one near enough to overhear."

This, of course, excluded the agog knife boys juggling with the cutlery.

"My darling," said Dumka. "Let us not cry over the broken vodka bottle. Tell me about Vienna. The affairs of the heart, they were amusing—yes?"

Dourakova considered. "Amusing—no," she said. "But I think you will agree that they were sensible. I have," she announced, "married Grisha."

"Grisha!" said Dumka surprised. "But he sleeps all the time," he objected.

"In a husband this is not altogether a disadvantage," said Dourakova. "Else I would not be having supper with you, my darling," she pointed out.

Dumka smoothed out his whiskers.

"And at his work he is a genius," said Dourakova. "Never

has my applause been so well organized. Seventeen curtains for Esmeralda and an encore for the thirty-two fouettés in Lac."

"An encore in Lac," said Dumka shocked. "It is not in the tradition."

"It is in Vienna," said Dourakova carelessly. She waved away Austria. "I tell you, my darling, there has never been a leader of the claque like my Grisha. When I marry him and bring him here, Chaliapin is in tears and Caruso come to plead personally with me. And even though he sing Pagliacci, I am adamant. So he has to employ instead Mario, who it is well known has no influence with the upper circle." She laughed merrily.

"A prudent marriage," said Dumka. "My congratulations."

"Prudent!" said Dourakova. "It is sheer genius this marriage. Listen to me, my Dumka," she turned her great eyes on him. "There are some ballerinas who marry their impresarios, there are others who marry their conductors—both of these are good for the career. There are the ballerinas that marry the business-men, but soon they cease to be ballerinas. There are the silly ones that marry other dancers, but these we need not discuss. But me," she boasted, "I am the first ballerina who has married her cheer-leader, and now am certain of what, au fond, is the most important thing in a ballerina's life—her applause."

She drank her champagne.

"You are the one ballerina in the world who does not need a claque," said Dumka, "but all the same," he admitted, "it is wise to have it."

He toasted her.

"And now," he said, "when shall we see you dance next?"

Dourakova put down her glass. "It is not when," she said. "It is where." She drooped a little.

"You have no definite plans?" asked Dumka hopefully.

"Oh, yes, I have plans," said Dourakova. "Very definite plans. Odessa, Sevastopol. Kharkov. And," she said with mounting venom, "Omsk."

"The provincial tour!" said Dumka aghast.

"Yes, my darling," said Dourakova sadly. "Your divine Doura is going on a tour of your bug-ridden provinces."

"But, my darling," pleaded Dumka, almost unable to believe his ears. "I cannot let you do this."

"I can do nothing else," said Dourakova. She looked across at Diaghilev. "I have been very silly."

Dumka was nearly in tears. Indeed, it was not until he remembered what he was here for that he brightened.

"My darling," he said, "you shall not dance in these preposterous provinces. I, your Dumka, promise you this. Omsk!" he said scornfully. He remembered something. "Odessa," he substituted.

Dourakova smiled through her tears. "You are very loyal, my Dumka, and I am touched. But do not distress yourself for me. It is not the great tragedy. I will go into exile, but only for a little while, and by the time I return there will have been quarrels at the Maryinsky—new quarrels—and I will allow them to persuade me to take my place again. And what Grisha can do with a claque at the Maryinsky," she saw a vision, "is nobody's business. I will yet," she prophesied, "die twice in Giselle."

"Three times," cried Dumka, carried away.

Caution returned to Dourakova. "Remember," she said, "that what I have told you is for your ears alone. To the world I go to the provinces because the whole of Russia it clamours for me."

"What do you take me for?" said Dumka hurt.

Dourakova patted his sleeve. "There, there," she said, "finish your champagne."

"Doura!" Dumka leant forward. "There is no need for you to go to the provinces. I, too, have had the success. I am now," he announced importantly, "artistic adviser to the Ballet Stroganoff."

Dourakova wrinkled her brow. Stroganoff! Where had she heard that name before.

"But it is the awful man who will not go away all afternoon," she remembered. "He is funny. I like him," she decided.

"He is a great man," said Dumka reverently. "A little obstinate, but a great man. Figure-toi, ma petite, he arrives from Omsk without one friend in the capital—save me. Every door is closed to him and he has no money at all save what his father will not give him. He has an ambitious wife and a nagging mamoushka-in-law, and everywhere they laugh at him, and nowhere will they help him, but his great heart pushes on, and every night his curtain ring up at the Boris Goudonov, and if the audiences are not large they are growing bigger, and if the performance is not perfect it is improving all the time. He will succeed that one, Doura, you will see. And," he finished, "I love him better than my brother. Much," he remembered.

"The Boris Goudonov?" asked Dourakova vaguely. "Where is this?"

"It is not in Sevastopol," said Dumka. "It is not even in Odessa. It is here," he flourished his hand, "in the capital. And, my darling, from the moment that you step on to the platform on the station we all live only that you should come and join us."

He leant back in his chair. He wasn't doing so badly, he thought.

Dourakova laughed merrily.

"Oh, my Dumka, always you make the little jokes. Me— join a company from Omsk!"

"It is better than dancing there," said Dumka.

The smile died out. But the laughter continued. With an offer pending this was no time for friendship.

"I think I shall cancel the tour, anyway," said Dourakova. "They want me in Berlin. And I have just had a letter from London for the Coliseum, but I think," she pouted, "it is too small."

"It is also a music hall," said Dumka nastily.

They glared at one another.

"You do not believe me," said Dourakova.

"I do not," said Dumka.

They glared again. Dumka recovered first.

"My darling," he said, "we have been very frank with each other all night. Let it continue so. You," he said, "are in the purée. We are in the bortsch. Come to us," he urged, "and we will all be in the caviar."

Dourakova tasted the idea. "How temptingly you put it," she said.

"Come, my darling," said Dumka. "Come and see our company. Afterwards you shall decide." He glanced at his wrist-watch. "We are still in time for the last ballet. Let us hope," he made the little joke, "that it is not Boadicea."

It was not Boadicea.

As the divine Dourakova and General Dumka took their places in the box, trumpets blared and four elephants stood on their hind-legs and waved their front ones.

The ballerina took her bow. She was a performing seal.

"Dear God," said Dourakova, "are we then at the circus?"

"Oui," said Dumka heavily.

*   *   *

Dourakova was divine, Doura was a veritable angel— but she was not reasonable. No! On the other hand—a circus! Tcha! What a difference did it make to a ballerina what happened at a theatre on the nights she was not dancing in it? A lot of difference, thought Dumka, trudging alone through the night.

He had come so near to success, too. In the droshky driving to the Boris Goudonov the contract was practically signed. Even the two harps for Lac des Cygnes—a permanent clause in any Dourakova contract—had been mooted and agreed. The little grandfather would have to pay for an extra one—that was all there was to it. Practically signed —excepting for her right to dismiss the conductor, if she did not approve of him, and that could have been settled by a little clause obligating her not to exercise this privilege unreasonably and a further little clause calling on her, should she so exercise it, to produce a new conductor mutually acceptable to all parties at a no greater salary. Ballerinas were child's play when you knew how to handle them. But this was an unmanageable child.

Dear Doura! Damn Doura! Where had he walked himself to?

No matter.

How to tell Stroganoff? How to tell the brave Vladimir of the failure of his mission? How to tell the brave little grandfather? If only he, Dumka, were a wealthy man! If only he had not gambled so much when he was young! If only he could win the State lottery! . . .

"Bon soir, mon général. You like the pretty lady?"

General Dumka stared at the mackintoshed figure that had loomed up in the night.

"I loathe the pretty lady," he said. "And," he sighed, "I adore her."

"How you like them?" pursued the mackintosh. "Plump?"

"No," said General Dumka. He shook his head. "I am too old, my friend." He prepared to walk on.

The mackintosh shrugged. "So be it," he said.

A white Homburg hat came sailing up through the night. The mackintosh bent itself double.

"Maestro," it breathed.

The white Homburg nodded vaguely and sailed on.

"That," said the mackintosh gazing after it in awed worship, "is the biggest white-slaver in Petersburg."

His ambitions rekindled. He grasped Dumka by the arm.

209

"You want the pretty lady," he urged. "Plump," he tempted.

The Wild Strawberry, Dancing and Singing, was one of several dozen similar establishments in the capital but happened to be the best in the neighbourhood. General Dumka furiously waving away the mackintosh whose pretty lady was getting plumper with every step, turned into it thankfully. It would at least serve as a refuge and the little drink would hearten him to break his sad news to the Stroganoffs, at the moment, no doubt, pacing the room—all three of them.

The Wild Strawberry was full of revellers sounding their chest notes, not all of them sober but all of them keeping pretty good time.

Particularly in the left-hand corner, where a bald dome was waving its arms at a gaunt face.

"I cannot live without champagne," it affirmed in a fruity baritone.

One of the Stroganoffs was not pacing the room.

General Dumka threaded his way through the smoke and the Otchi Tchernias.

"Vladimir," he said accusingly, "why are you singing?"

"Dumka!" Stroganoff, a bright pink moon of affability embraced him. "My dear Dumka. Come—sing with us. Two Guitars," he commanded his neighbours.

"Two Guitars," agreed Grisha. He began it.

Dumka chafed impatiently while the Leader of the Claque organized the room through three choruses.

"Vladimir!" He seized on the lull. "I bring bad news."

"To-night no news is bad," said Stroganoff. "Gaida Troika," he suggested.

"As you will," said Grisha. He mounted the table.

"No, no," said Dumka. "Vladimir—listen to me. Dourakova will not come to us."

"Is that all!" Stroganoff thumped Dumka on the back. "My friend, you distress yourself for nothing. She has no choice. To-night," he pointed to the crescendoing Grisha, "I have signed up her cheer-leader."

"Gaida Troika!" roared the swaying, waving, carried-away room.

"See," said Stroganoff, "he is in great form."

General Dumka sat down. He considered the situation.

"Gaida Troika," he joined in, much relieved.

AND that," Stroganoff told the sandy man, "was the beginning of the turning-tide. From this moment things begin to change for me."

"About time," said the sandy man.

"For," said Stroganoff, "after the argument marital with the leader of the claque, the seventeen aspirins, and the little weep on Dumka's shoulder, Dourakova sign with the ballet Stroganoff a contract that run into twenty-four pages, and I am the coming man."

"Hallo, Vladimir. Ça va, mon vieux?"

"Ça va," said the coming man, beaming.

Vladimir Stroganoff was taking his morning stroll down the Nevsky Prospekt, though it was not so much a stroll as a royal progress. Ever since Dourakova had signed people had hailed him instead of pointing at him. Invitations to dinner parties, gambling parties, singing parties, which he did not answer, snowed into his letter-box. Photographers offered him free sittings, all of which he accepted. Dukes and Duchesses bowed to him, and only little Ginsberg scurried to the other side of the street at his approach— that one had troubles enough.

"And as things changed for me," Stroganoff told the sandy man, "so they changed for Diaghilev."

"He found money?" asked the sandy man.

"He found courage," said Stroganoff. "He decided to open in Paris without State backing and hope for the best. If I am correctly informed," said Stroganoff, "he did not settle for the scenery till many years later."

Aliosha and the little grandfather, the former pushing the latter, came in for their share of adulation. For the first time Aliosha kissed the hand of a grand-duchess and the little grandfather was called an international financier, which was not what they had called him in the old days.

"In fact," Stroganoff told the sandy man, "in those days that preceded Dourakova's opening there was but one cloud on the horizon. My wife."

"You sleep alone?" asked the sandy man, smiling indulgently.

"Not always," said Stroganoff. "But I do not sleep with my Natasha. She is still in my company, but we are not more to one another than the newest little choryphée. Less," he remembered.

"And the opening was a success then?" asked the sandy man.

"My friend," said Stroganoff irritated. "Who tells this story? You or me?"

Conseille de famille—most of it. But instead of Natasha and the mamoushka, there were Dourakova and the leader of the claque.

"Stroganoff," said Dourakova, "listen."

Three heads turned sharply.

"We have been talking delicately long enough," said Dourakova. "Let us get down to facts." She announced the first one. "Your company is terrible."

"My company!" Vladimir was on his feet.

"Our company!" Aliosha's stomach heaved.

"Silence—both of you," said the little grandfather. "It is possible that the woman is talking sense. It is not often that a woman talks sense, but in this case," he stated, "I have an instinct that she may be right."

"I am right," said Dourakova. "Mind you," she said fairly, "every ballet company is terrible, but the difference between the good and the bad company is that the good has learnt how to conceal the terrible. You," she denounced emphatically, "take all your worst points and bring them to the front."

"My Katusha," said Aliosha thoughtfully. He dismissed the dreadful suspicion.

"Consider your leading dancer," said Dourakova. "He is no Nijinsky, we are agreed. Then why," she demanded, "do you give him what only Vatza can do?"

"But since we give the ballet," objected Vladimir, "someone has to dance it."

"Then you do not give that ballet," said Dourakova. "That is the whole point. You must stay within the limitations of your company. That," she said firmly, "is what I will insist on as long as I am with it."

"But you have no limitations, my darling," said General Dumka.

The leader of the claque looked surprised.

"If I could dance all evening I would," said Dourakova.
"Believe me I would. But I must have support—every
dancer must have support—and," she emphasized, "it must
be the right support. So, Vladimir," she turned on him, "you
can tear up the ambitious programme you have composed
for my opening, for it would take the whole of the Maryinsky
and Diaghilev working together and staying like that to
achieve it."

"But . . ." said Vladimir.

"Silence," said the little grandfather. "You heard what
she told you. Tear it up."

With sulky determination Vladimir ripped.

"I have thought over the programme carefully," said
Dourakova. "The opening ballet shall be something slight
and it shall be without me. I would suggest Snegourotchka.
It is not too difficult and your wife will be very charming
in it."

"Not to me," said Vladimir.

"For my first ballet," said Dourakova, "I will do the
second act of Lac."

"Lac," said Vladimir unhappily. "Natasha has been dancing Lac."

"Exactly," said Dourakova, "and that is the sort of thing
that has got to stop. Also," she discovered, "I shall require
Natasha to lead the Swans. With Arenskaya," she added,
"they will not be at all bad," she said generously.

"Oh," said Vladimir. He was visualizing himself telling
them.

"We will end with Divertissement," said Dourakova.

"Here we will give such of your company as merit it a chance."

"Katusha," said Aliosha. But he said it under his breath.

"I," said Dourakova, "will do the Sugar Plum variation, and that conductor will go through it with me and he will get it right or . . . What is the clause, my darling?"

Grisha opened his eyes. "Elevenb," he said. He closed them again.

"And so," Stroganoff told the sandy man, "I announce the programme for the opening. And at once all the seats are booked and I am in the roubles. And then the rehearsals begin and it seems as if a miracle had happen to my company."

He looked at Pavlova's portrait.

"Yes, my friend, a miracle. The presence of Dourakova acted as a spur to my loyal little company. For her they could achieve what before they had never dared to attempt. Figurez-vous, mon vieux, Kashkavar Jones achieve four turns where before he had done but one and a half and faked. Success," said Stroganoff, "was in the air."

"And your wife?" asked the sandy man.

"My wife," Stroganoff sighed. "She was an aloof stranger. When I gave her Snegourotchka all she said was 'very well,' and she hold up her hand to silence the mamoushka."

"And Arenskaya?" asked the sandy man.

Stroganoff smiled. "Doura, she have the little word with Arenskaya."

"You are the divine Dourakova," shrilled Arenskaya.

"Bon. You have come here to save the company. Bon! You are the greatest artist the world has ever seen. Bon! But if you criticize my behind once more," she quivered, "I slap your face."

Dourakova gazed at her serenely. "You should not stick it out," she said.

A rattle-snake deciding where to strike next, Árenskaya drew back.

"And it is for this that I walk out of the Maryinsky," she found. "To have my behind criticized by a ballerina who has only just not shown her own—much bigger—to Nijni Novgorod."

For a second Dourakova's eyes became slits of ice. She controlled herself. She could be as shrill as anybody, but this was not the time.

"My little one," she said, "you were rash to leave the Maryinsky on, shall we say, an impulse. There at least there was no chance that they would give you to do what you could not do."

"That you should tell me this," said Arenskaya scornfully. "You, who walked out, not on an impulse but after arguing for seven months."

"I am Dourakova," said Dourakova. She looked up as though waiting for the trumpets to sound in heaven.

"And me, I am Arenskaya," said Arenskaya.

No trumpets.

"Not yet," said Dourakova with deadly gentleness. "Though you may well be when I have finished with you. You have temperament," she conceded, "but you must learn to control it. And your behind. You can be Arenskaya when you are older," she smiled, "and can remember your triumphs to pupils too young to have known them."

"Me a teacher!" Arenskaya was aghast.

"In time," said Dourakova. "In time you will almost certainly end up as a teacher. And so," she discovered a little sadly, "will I."

Abashed by this glimpse of the future, Arenskaya's fury ebbed.

"In the meantime," said Dourakova, blinking back her own tears, "control your behind."

"And so," Stroganoff told the sandy man, "to the opening night."

The opening night.

The Boris Goudonov was one vast flutter of programmes. The audience rocked on its feet, glittering, glowing, and acclaiming. Grand Duchesses forgot themselves and not a monocle remained in place.

"Dourakova! Dourakova! Dourakova!"

A great ballerina was restored to her own.

"Dourakova! Dourakova! Dourakova!"

Grisha had done his job well.

In a box Prince Volkonsky tapped Teleyakov on a sulky shoulder.

"You should never have allowed her to leave us," he said for the eleventh time that evening. "After all," he argued, "what are a few insults from a dancer."

Above her flowers Dourakova bowed, smiled, and blinked back her tears. And the house would not let her go.

"Dourakova! Dourakova! Dourakova!"

In the wings Natasha and her mamoushka stood listening.

"Six curtains," said Natasha. "Six curtains."

". . . Seven," said the mamoushka.

". . . And eight," said Natasha, ". . . and nine."

". . . And ten," said the mamoushka.

"I can't bear it," sobbed Natasha. She fled to her dressing-room.

". . . And eleven," shouted the mamoushka after her.

"And that night the Students carried Dourakova shoulder high all the way to the Cubat," Stroganoff told the sandy man. "And me," he laughed, "I was a student, too." He rubbed his shoulder reminiscently.

The Cubat was crowded out. And when the orchestra played Lac des Cygnes to welcome the ballerina's entrance, the world of fashion stood up to cheer.

And Grisha nowhere in sight.

It took Stroganoff a quarter of an hour to steer his star past the tables insisting on toasting her. And when they reached the forty couverts of their own company, Arenskaya came forward and kissed the great ballerina on the cheek.

"You were right," she said. "You are Dourakova."

"And Natasha?" asked the sandy man.

"Natasha looked radiant," said Stroganoff. "And she presented Dourakova with the diamond bracelet, and she embraced her and she embraced me. Never would you have guessed to look at her that in her bag was a letter to Paris she had written but a few moments ago." Stroganoff looked at the window. "To Diaghilev," he said.

CHAPTER XXI

A MADDENING morning at the Maryinsky.

Kshessinskaya had left for Paris to join Diaghilev. Measles had broken out in the school. Once again Pavlova was talking of forming her own company. And now, to crown it all, a crested command from Tzarskoe Selo.

Dourakova! The Emperor would pick this morning to pick Dourakova!

Teleyakov signed to his secretary.

"Send for the man from Omsk," he said distastefully.

A wonderful morning in Theatre Street. The man from Omsk strolled down it wondering how long it would take him to own the place. The director of the State Theatres had sent for him—no doubt to ask his advice. Well, he would have plenty of suggestions to make. There was room for improvement at the Maryinsky. That patch on the carpet in the vestibule, for instance. Were they going to offer him a directorate? On the whole he thought he might accept.

"M'sieur, your carte d'entrée?"

Stroganoff flourished it. "See," he said, "to-day I do not

have to offer you the little bribe." But all the same, he passed the sentry five roubles.

The sentry stared after him. It was not the same sentry. But Stroganoff was already strolling towards the class-room.

Class at the Maryinsky.

Preobrajenska, Egorova, Trefilova. And a lot of others.

"Pas mal," said Stroganoff indulgently. "Pas mal du tout." He looked around. "No Pavlova! You should not allow her to do this," he told the about-to-overboil maestro. He ran a finger along the mantelpiece. "Clean," he said surprised. He sauntered out.

A secretary hurried up. "Prince Teleyakov is waiting," he murmured behind his hand.

"I will be up in a moment," promised Stroganoff gazing out of the window at the regimented geraniums beneath. "Ah," he sighed, "if I could but get my girls in line like this. Who is your head gardener, my friend?" he enquired.

*　　*　　*

"Come in," said Teleyakov unnecessarily.

"Bon jour, mon ami," said Stroganoff with warmth. He looked round the walls. Not enough photographs and none of them signed. Yes—plenty of changes to make!

"Sit down," said Teleyakov too late. "Cigarette," he offered only just in time.

"I thank you," said Stroganoff. He inspected it. No monogram!

"Vladimir Alexandrovitch," said Teleyakov, "you are no doubt surprised that I have sent for you."

"Surprised?" Stroganoff tasted the idea. "No," he decided, "I am not saying that I am surprised. Is it not natural that one impresario should seek the advice of another? Now that I am the success all day long, people ask for my advice. And the little loan," he remembered. "The advice I give them."

"Indeed," said Teleyakov.

"Why only yesterday," said Stroganoff, "the Grand Duchess ask me to approve her mayonnaise and poof, suddenly I am in the kitchen and the French chef is very cross. And this morning he leave for Paris." He passed on to happier topics. "You have slept well—no?"

Teleyakov inclined a slightly bewildered head.

"Me, I do not sleep at all," said Stroganoff. "First I am not in bed till five and then I have the troubles marital, and as well as this there are the many problems that the successful impresario must consider each day."

You're telling me, looked Teleyakov.

"I am the success you assure me," said Stroganoff. "Entendu! But this does not settle everything and my finance," he admitted, "is still the rickets. You like to hear about my overhead?" he offered.

"It is fantastic I am sure," said Teleyakov dryly. Would he never be permitted to come to the point?

"And yet we economize everywhere," said Stroganoff. "The water in the fountain, it play in the intervals only."

"Ah," said Teleyakov. He made a note.

"The business is enormous," said Stroganoff, "but so are the debts, and the profits they must go to pay for the lean years."

"Years?" said Teleyakov.

"Months, weeks, days," said Stroganoff. "Why you quibble?"

Teleyakov raised a protesting hand. "M'sieur," he said, "shall we come to business?"

Stroganoff spread himself more comfortably in his armchair. "But it is for this that I am here," he assured Teleyakov. "Time, as my little grandfather says, is money—may he live for ever. And now I am all attention." He sighted a portrait on the wall. "Who is that?" he asked.

"His Imperial Majesty," said Teleyakov coldly.

"Sir," said Teleyakov, "you are a very obstinate man."

It was half an hour later. Teleyakov partly by mesmerism, and partly by lung power, but mainly by Russian tea and pirojki, had got Stroganoff silent for long enough to state his business.

"The Tzar has commanded that the dancer Dourakova appear at Tzarskoe Selo. He has not," said Teleyakov warmly, "commanded your company."

"It is implied," said Stroganoff. He munched. "A ballerina does not appear without a company."

"The Maryinsky Theatre can supply all the dancers required," said Teleyakov. "It has done so for more than a century."

"But it cannot supply Dourakova," said Stroganoff unmoved. "She is under contract to me." He looked at the empty plate. "Finished," he said sorrowfully.

With superb self-control Teleyakov rang for more.

"Vladimir Alexandrovitch," he said. "Think very carefully. It is a great privilege for you, a provincial, with but one season in the capital, to be permitted to present your star at Tzarskoe Selo. Do not be too obstinate or," he lied, "I can easily suggest to the Emperor that he ask someone else."

"If you can do this," said Stroganoff, quaking inwardly but bluffing hard, "then I suggest that you go to work at once, for," he dug his chin in the air, "Dourakova goes to Tzarskoe Selo with my company or she goes not at all. Ah— the pirojki!" He stretched out a hand.

Teleyakov looked at the munching figure. "You are as obstinate as Diaghilev," he declared, "and like Diaghilev you will have to learn your lesson."

Stroganoff shivered.

"But for the moment," said Teleyakov, "you get your own way. Take your confounded company to Tzarskoe Selo." Just in time he snatched the last pirojki.

"Cabbage!" he snorted.

A maddening day.

"And so that night after the performance," Stroganoff told the sandy man, "I call the company on the stage for the announcement tremendous. . . ."

"My children," said Stroganoff. "Have I done well for you?"

A chorus of acclamation arose from the assembled Omskites.

"Papa Stroganoff!" "Papa Stroganoff!" "Well done!"

Stroganoff blushed and beamed and swelled out and

blew his nose and opened wide his eyes. To be acclaimed as the father of a ballet company at the age of twenty-seven —this was indeed an achievement!

The meeting was being held on the dismembered vastnesses of the stage of the Boris Goudonov, with only a very sleepy wedged-in-the-corner elephant and a yawning of stage hands looking on.

"The Tzar!" breathed Katusha.

"Tzarskoe Selo," marvelled Little Igor. "Me—at Tzarskoe Selo."

"It will not be so big as the Palace Buckingham," said Kashkavar Jones, "which," he remembered, "is built of solid gold so the sentries have to guard it day and night."

"The Company Stroganoff at the Emperor's summer palace," gloated Nevajno's best friend. "Hurrah!" He thought of something. "No scheques," he said warningly.

Nevajno stopped beaming.

"A command performance for Dourakova," said Dourakova. "I thank you, Vladimir. It was well arranged."

"The credit, my darling, goes to you," said Stroganoff gallantly. "But me also," he hurried on, "I have done my share. Who was it brought the company from Omsk?" he demanded. "Me! Who was it kept the faith burning bright when all looked dark? Me!" he chanted. "Who was it who beg, who borrow, and who keep the credit good? Me!" He thumped his chest. "And when everybody say this man from Omsk is the kaput, who was it persuade you, my darling," he turned and beamed on Dourakova, "to join us?"

"Dumka," said Dourakova.

"Me!" gloried Stroganoff. "And who is now the most

successful impresario in the capital with the back salaries nearly paid off? Me!" he triumphed. "Me!"

"Papa Stroganoff. Papa Stroganoff!" cheered the company.

From the dim recesses of his childhood memories Kashkavar Jones burst into song.

"For he's a jolly good sparrow," he carolled.

That night it was Stroganoff who was chained to the Cubat.

"But before all this happen," Stroganoff told the sandy man, "Natasha comes to see me in my office."

"Stroganoff," said Natasha, "I have something to tell you."

With some difficulty Stroganoff prevented himself from embracing her. His little wife and such wonderful news he had to give her! But no, he remembered. An intransigent member of his company.

"What can I do for you?" he said formally.

Natasha passed him a letter. "It is from Diaghilev," she said. "He has enclosed my fare to Paris."

"So," said Stroganoff. He put on his spectacles.

"It is not that I want to leave you, Vladimir," said Natasha embarrassed. "You do what you can. But my career . . . With you, instead of going forward it is going back."

Stroganoff put away his spectacles. "Little idiot," he said, "is it 'going back' to dance at Tzarskoe Selo before the Tzar?"

"Tzarskoe Selo!" Natasha was confused.

"Oui," said Stroganoff. "The Ballet Stroganoff dances for the Tzar."

The colour came into Natasha's cheeks. "But this is wonderful," she began. "Vladimir . . ." She stopped.

"I congratulate you," she said. "It is a great thing for the Ballet Stroganoff. But what difference can it make to me? It is Dourakova who will dance before the Tzar. Stroganova, she will support Dourakova."

"Bien sûr," said a brisk voice from the doorway.

Dourakova came in. She beamed at Stroganoff and put an arm round Natasha. "And very prettily she will support her, too," she said.

"Mademoiselle Stroganova is leaving the company to join Diaghilev," said Stroganoff in what he hoped was an icy voice.

"What nonsense is this?" said Dourakova. "And at such a moment!" She settled herself comfortably in Stroganoff's chair. "Listen, my child. You have been loyal to the company through the bad times—stay now and enjoy the good."

"Good!" said Natasha. "For whom?"

"But for all of us," said Dourakova. "For me, for you, and for our dear Vladimir, who kills himself for love of you."

Stroganoff tried to look like an impresario. But he only looked like a husband.

"For all of us," he echoed.

"For you, Vladimir, yes," said Natasha. "For Dourakova certainly. Dourakova will get the diamond cipher from the Tzar. But Stroganova," her lips were thin, "Stroganova will not even get her six curtains."

"Curtains?" said Dourakova. "What is this about curtains?"

"My life is a nightmare for her six curtains," exploded Stroganoff. "They break my marriage and they spoil my company—her six curtains. It would take a book to explain about her six curtains. But enfin," he told Dourakova, "she will not be happy until she has her six curtains and at Tzarskoe Selo she sees no hope, so she goes to Diaghilev. Bon," he said exhausted. "So be it. I have wept too much already." He folded his arms.

But Dourakova only smiled. "Then she shall have her six curtains," she said. "Why not?" She patted Natasha's shoulder. "Do not worry, my little one—we will arrange it."

Natasha seemed unable to believe her ears. "Six curtains at Tzarskoe Selo! You are not teasing me?"

"No, no," said Dourakova. "You shall have them."

Six curtains at Tzarskoe Selo. Natasha looked at Dourakova. She looked at her suddenly hopeful husband. She burst into tears.

"There, there," said Dourakova. "You do not have to thank me." She patted the weeping back. "You are very pretty and we will find you a solo not too difficult, and, enfin, six curtains it is not so many. I," she decided, "will have sixteen."

"Sssh," said Stroganoff urgently.

*　　*　　*

"I am so happy the night my company chair me to the Cubat," Stroganoff told the sandy man. "The Tzar commands my Ballet, my wife does not go to Diaghilev, Almire gives me the best table in the room, Pavlova bows to me," he looked at the portrait with tears in his eyes. "Teleyakov nods. And the band it play 'The Conquering Hero from Omsk' . . ."

It was three o'clock in the morning. Someone was tapping at Stroganoff's bedroom door.

"Qui c'est," called Stroganoff urgently.

"It is me," said a diffident little voice. "Natasha. Vladimir —can I come in?"

Stroganoff tumbled out of bed.

"Un petit moment," he called from one side of his mouth. "The other door," he hissed from the other side of his mouth. "Quick! Quick!"

The newest little choryphée scuttled.

"And next morning," Stroganoff told the sandy man, "I have a new pair of cuff links. A present from Natasha. See I wear them still." He shot his cuffs. "And in my ears I hear Diaghilev whistle for his fare all the way from Paris."

CHAPTER XXII

Aℕᴅ now," said Stroganoff, "we come to the cornerstone of my career. Pancakes! Delicious!"

The sandy man looked at him.

"Pancakes from the Tzaritza," explained Stroganoff. "Served with her own hands on a gold plate just as though we were the Maryinsky. I have one still," he said reverently.

"What?" exclaimed the sandy man.

"It is the souvenir," said Stroganoff. "Nevajno omit to give his back. The gold plate," he explained.

"Snitched it," said the sandy man.

"Not at all," said Stroganoff warmly. "Nevajno is a genius. He does not snitch, he omits only to give back." He flicked his ash on to the desk. He looked at it. "Where," he demanded, "is my silver ash-tray?"

"Your genius put it in his pocket," said the sandy man.

"Aie! My solid silver presentation in Nevajno's pocket," cried Stroganoff. "I must stop him quick before he take it out by accident at the pawnbrokers."

He lifted the receiver and spoke furiously in Russian. The receiver spoke back.

"It is all right," said Stroganoff, hanging up. "Arenskaya

she go chase him. But the trouble I shall have to get it back from Arenskaya. . . . No matter." He dismissed the subject. "Where were we, my friend . . ."

"Pancakes," said the sandy man.

"You smile, my friend," said Stroganoff, "but the pancakes were the most important part of any presentation of the Ballet at the palace. The pancakes and the gold watch for the dancer and the Tzar's initial in a diamond cipher brooch for the ballerina. My friend," Stroganoff sighed, "they say many evil things of our poor dead Tzar, but to the ballet he was the little father. There is a ballet in Leningrad now and it dances for the people, and it is a very good thing that the people should see the ballet and I would be the last to say anything against it, in fact, I dream that one day my company will dance there, too. But it will not be the same thing, my friend, it will not be the same thing at all." He looked at Pavlova's portrait and it seemed as though she were mourning with him because something had gone from a world where there was no Tzaritza to serve pancakes to the ballet with her own hands.

"Stalin is a great man," said Stroganoff, "and all of us are learning to love him. It will give me great pleasure that he will come to my box and watch the ballet and maybe send for me. But," he faced it, "I do not see him giving out the pancakes on golden plates."

He blew his nose.

"Yes," he said, "our Tzar was the father of his ballet. And whether he was in his winter palace or his summer palace or at any other palace, he would send for the dancers he wished to see. Sometimes it was the great stars of the State

Theatre, sometimes it was the little children studying in the State schools, sometimes it was a foreign ballerina who had come to the capital, and once it was the Ballet Stroganoff. This they cannot take from me." He thumped the desk. "Whatever the critics say of my ballet, they cannot take from me that once I am sent for at Tzarskoe Selo. Me!"

The sandy man maintained a tactful silence.

"My friend," said Stroganoff, "in this country you, too, have the many emotions when your King send for you at the Buckingham Palace or the Castle Windsor. The glory is perhaps the same, but the costume," he raised his hands, "is very different."

"Ah, well," said the sandy man.

"My company at Tzarskoe Selo," transported Stroganoff. "My friend, you have watched your little debutantes going to make their curtsies to your King. The anticipations, the preparations, the palpitations! My friend, I tell you, my whole company it is the little debutante."

The palpitations!

The Company Stroganoff was one mass of curling irons, smoothing irons, goffering irons, and all sorts of other irons —all of them in the fire. Never had there been such a profusion of preparation. Never had so many dancing daughters had their faces slapped by so many *énervées* mamoushkas. Kashkavar Jones, that staunch Anglomane, had dwindled Tzarskoe Selo to a lodge in Windsor Park while madly brushing his tunic, Little Igor had gambled all night to win back his overcoat, only to find that its last winner had cut short the cuffs, and Stroganoff was even now standing in front of a mirror tying and retying his white butterfly in a mounting wail of self-criticism.

"Son of my son," said Moysha, "the Tzar will not be looking at your tie."

"We cannot be certain of this," said Aliosha. He pushed his son to one side, stood in front of the mirror, and twiddled.

"When I used to go to Tzarskoe Selo," said Moysha, "I did not even trouble to change my costume." He shook his head at his carnation.

"Little grandfather," said Vladimir, "this is the first time you go in by the front door."

The little grandfather hobbled to the mirror and pushed his son out of the way. He, too, twiddled.

The carriages of the Tzar await!

They had drawn up outside the Boris Goudonov, the outriders slithering, the coaches clattering, the harness bells ringing—an impressive formation, the horses with the sheen that only a royal stable can give and the uniforms of the postillions glittering in the setting sun.

"They're here!" An excited mamoushka ran out on to the steps and ran in again.

"They're here!" Masses of people ran out on to the steps and ran in again.

And now the Ballet Stroganoff proceeded to transfer itself, encouraged by the advice of every small boy in the neighbourhood. First the heavy baskets of costumes and the harps. Then the choryphées to the rear carriages with here and there a mamoushka, carrying a wicker basket with personal props—tinsel roses, false curls, and every ballet shoe she could lay her hands on. Then the soloists, Arenskaya swinging her hips, and Natasha, an angel from an Easter cake, escorting them. No Nijinsky, very pale and quiet, and Kashkavar Jones, talking loudly of King Edward's marriages of gold and rubies, and Little Igor, trying to keep his wrists in his sleeve.

Then Aliosha, Moysha, and Natasha's mamoushka in a state of temporary truce.

"Old woman," trebled Moysha. "If I were a horse I'd eat that hat."

Very temporary.

A carriage for Dourakova and her roses. Somewhere between the blooms the bald dome of Stroganoff, shining as pink as any of them.

If only Diaghilev could see him now his cup would be full and a gold cup at that.

A horseman came jogging into the square. He was covered with medals. On closer inspection he turned out to be General Dumka.

"Courage, mon vieux," he called. "Bonne chance, mes amis. I will be with you in the audience." He reined himself nearer to Dourakova's carriage. "But in order to do this," he explained, "I must start."

His horse nodded, and still together they jogged happily away.

And now the very last straggler clambered into her carriage.

The head coachman waved his whip, the outriders shot away. Chased by the furiously twinkling feet of every small boy in the neighbourhood, the procession moved off.

"My darling," Dourakova's small hand stole into Stroganoff's podgy one. "My darling, you will hardly believe this but," said the great ballerina, "I am feeling very nervous."

"You will hardly believe it," said her impresario, clutching her fingers tightly, "but me, too."

"You will hardly believe it," said the cheer-leader to Nicholas Nevajno, who wasn't listening, "but I am very nervous. To lead the cheers when one has no claque to instruct but only generals, who cannot be trusted not to applaud everyone—this is a project very delicate."

"Divertissement!" said Nevajno, which was all he had been allowed to devise. "Pfui!"

"For Doura it is simple," said the cheer-leader. "She has but to dance and her responsibility is at an end."

"Divertissement!" said Nevajno. "I offer Vladimir my new choreographic conception, 'The Revolution,' very realistic —but Vladimir he say 'Wait for it.' "

"And six curtains for Stroganova," said the cheer-leader. "It is an order. But how I am to execute it only the good God knows. If He does," he doubted.

"I have brought with me my scheque book," said Nevajno bleakly, "but I do not hope to find the heart to bring it out. . . ."

★   ★   ★

In the Gold Room at the Summer Palace they had erected a stage. Its crimson curtain bore the Royal cipher and the proscenium arch held the Imperial Eagle's outstretched wings. But what was going on behind it closely resembled what went on behind any other proscenium just before a performance—catastrophe and confusion. Exhaustion and hopefulness. And worse.

For it is easy enough to chase off an ordinary small boy, who has managed to insert himself into the wings of a theatre and is taking an active interest in the preparations. But it is much less simple when the small boy happens to be the heir to the throne of Russia.

"Shoo, Highness," said Vladimir Stroganoff. "Shoo," he added pleadingly.

"Highness," begged Aliosha. "Where is your nurse?"

"Don't know," said the Tzarevitch. "Don't care." He poised a nail on a plank and reached for a hammer.

"Little boy run away," trebled Moysha. "Highness," he remembered.

A nurse came rushing across the stage, snatched the Tzarevitch from the nail, and held him to her brocaded bosom.

"Highness—thank God I was in time." She turned on the Stroganoffs. "You should be under arrest," she snapped. "The lot of you. Nails indeed! Don't you know what happens if his Highness cuts himself?"

She tucked his Highness under her sturdy arms and waddled off, suffering his kicks with a detachment that could only speak of long practice.

The Stroganoffs groaned. They knew what would happen if his Highness cut himself. The whole of Russia knew that the Tzarevitch would bleed to death, that the doctors could do nothing, that only one man in all the land could master the child and stop the flow of blood with his blessed herbs.

Rasputin.

The Stroganoffs mopped their brows. Practically on their way to Siberia!

★   ★   ★

The Gold Room at Tzarskoe Selo was gold. So was the throne. Even the chairs were backed by golden eagles. The ceiling was encrusted with semi-precious stones, the pillars were amethyst and amber, and the great candelabras rivalled anything that could be found in Versailles.*

And in this room the guests began to assemble—so much blue blood trapped out in so much bejewelled splendour! Princes and Dukes (for there were none of lower rank save the Foreign Ambassadors and Embassy riff-raff), wearing ceremonial uniforms, and Princesses and Duchesses in the bejewelled brocades of their ancestors with stiff resplendent head-dresses, moving to their inherited places to form two long shining lines, awaiting the entry of the Emperor in a perfection of etiquette on which what sun would ever dare to set? How could anything on the other side of the footlights equal what was going on before them?

" 'Pon my soul," said Bingo Haymarket, the young attaché to the British Ambassador, "and they told me the beggars were savages."

"So they are," said the British Ambassador, his face not moving a muscle.

The lines shivered and glinted like steppe-land corn in

---

* Now buy the film rights!

the sun and the wind. Princesses and Duchesses sank to the ground. Ambassadors and attachés inclined their heads. The little father of all the Russias was coming in.

Tzar and Tzaritza advanced to the throne. Behind them was Rasputin, with unkempt hair, and food-stained tunic, his hands two dirty claws.

"Well, I'm damned," said Bingo Haymarket under his breath. Suddenly he felt homesick for Sandringham.

★   ★   ★

The lights in the chandeliers faded away. The footlights glowed up. The first bars of Tchaikowsky swept through the room.

It might have been a real theatre.

Behind the curtain the collective stomach of the Stroganoff Ballet Company turned over.

"The rest is with God," said Vladimir Stroganoff. He sat down on a packing-case beside his father and his father's father.

"My son," said Aliosha heavily. "I am wishing I was in Omsk where there is only Abram to say we stink."

"Be silent, both of you," said the little grandfather. He put on his hat and muttered a prayer in Hebrew. If anything went wrong now it would be his fault for sipping that glass of tea on Yom Kippur.

The overture was nearing its end. On the stage a bunch of turning-over stomachs had sorted themselves into a graceful group. How cold they were! How their outstretched arms trembled. If only this were Omsk!

In the wings Natasha's stomach sank into her toes, rose

239

to her throat, then sank again. But the stomach of Arenskaya pulled itself together, though her knees went on shaking.

"Come," she said. "We are not frightened—us! Look at
Doura," she exhorted. "See how calm she is!"

The calm Dourakova forced her knocking knees to carry
her over to Natasha.

"For once I envy you, my child," she said. "You are dancing first, and it will be the sooner over."

The curtain went up.

On the stage shivering arms stiffened, quaking knees became rocks. Their Tzar was looking at them!

"Bonne chance," whispered Dourakova. "Remember all
that you have to do is dance."

Crossing herself furiously, Natasha's mamoushka stumbled over to the Stroganoffs.

"Vladimir," she begged. "Pray with me." She extended
her hand. Vladimir grasped it. For the first time they were
in complete sympathy.

The difference between a good ballet company and a bad
ballet company, Dourakova had said, is that the good has
learnt to conceal the terrible.

The Ballet Stroganoff had learned this lesson well. The
opening ballet was a dainty affair of buttercups and daisies
to the music of Mendelssohn, with Natasha as a butterfly
having her day. Dourakova had resuscitated it from an
older programme and Nevajno's suggestion of a spider who
would eat the butterfly had been firmly waved away.

As a butterfly, Natasha had no limitations. Never a piece

of Dresden china that she could not have adorned without comment, a combination of porcelain and purity that none could resist. Crouching in the musicians' gallery the cheer-leader relaxed. This assignment was not going to be so impossible after all.

In the wings, Dourakova nodded approvingly, the Stroganoffs were swelling every moment, and the mamoushka had decided it was safe to stop praying and had started to weep.

On the stage the butterfly's day was nearly spent. She fluttered weakly but deliciously. She went into a wide spin, not too fast and getting slower and slower until at last she sank to the ground amidst the mourning buttercups and the despairing daisies and to a frightening silence.

"Dear God!" panicked Natasha.

And then the Tzar nodded approvingly and the Tzaritza clapped.

And then the generals, who had only just managed to wait for it, applauded loudly. And then the whole Court joined in.

Radiant now, Natasha dropped a deep curtsey. The generals went on clapping. Natasha bowed and bowed.

Up in the musicians' gallery the cheer-leader dropped his unneeded hands.

"Pfui!" he said, "I have been wasting my time."

Six curtains for Natasha.

The first curtain was all that a curtain should be.

For one thing it came down slowly and gave the company plenty of time to line up, curtsey deeply to the Tzar, bow radiantly to the audience, and politely at one another. And the Court applauded warmly. After all, Tzarskoe Selo had sent for worse companies than this—once or twice.

The second curtain belonged to the butterfly. Natasha took it alone. The Tzaritza was only nodding approvingly, but the Tzar was still clapping.

By the third curtain the Tzar was nodding approvingly. But the generals went on clapping.

As it came down a small boy in an English sailor suit joined the Stroganoffs in the wings.

"I have come back," he announced. "Where is my hammer?" He wandered off looking for it.

"Aie!" said the Stroganoffs.

By the fourth curtain the going was heavier. For one thing the Stroganoffs were too preoccupied to help.

"Highness," pleaded Vladimir. "Not the nail. See—I have the sugar plum!" He fumbled in his pocket. Oh, why had he eaten them all?

The fifth curtain brought out the bouquets. The applause took on a fresh lease of life.

"Pretty lady," said the Tzarevitch, sighting the radiant butterfly. "I will give her some flowers." He pounced on a shield of roses due to be presented to Dourakova, dodged Vladimir's frantic grab at his blouse and ran on to the stage.

The applause stopped dead. The Tzar rose. The Tzaritza put her hand to her heart.

"Flowers for the pretty lady," said the Tzarevitch, struggling to hold up the shield so much larger than himself.

And then he dropped it and was sucking his thumb.

Pandemonium!

Doctors leapt to their feet, niankas streamed on to the stage. Generals turned pale and trembled, the Tzar was shouting and the Tzaritza was beating her breast.

The Sleeping Princess wasn't in it!

Bingo Haymarket dropped his monocle. "What's going on?" he asked.

The Tzarevitch looked up. Hundreds of anxious faces swarming round. Clearly a tantrum was in order. He opened his mouth and gave of his best.

And Natasha Stroganova stood unnoticed in the middle of her flowers. Five curtains, and the butterfly's day was spent.

*   *   *

In the end Rasputin consented to attend the child, as he always did when he thought the Tzaritza had wept long enough, and he picked him up in his arms and carried him to his vast uncosy nursery, and he stopped the bleeding with his blessed herbs and he calmed the child—he was the only man in Holy Russia who could.

And after they had sent the Nianka to Siberia, and after she had pleaded herself back, only slightly perturbed, for she knew the Tzarevitch would tolerate no other nurse, and after the Tzaritza had seen her son sleeping for herself, and dried her eyes and taken a sedative, and after the Tzar had taken a little something else, and everybody had given thanks to God, the performance was resumed.

The curtain went up. The ballet went on. The Stroganoffs could breathe again.

*   *   *

The divine Dourakova in Lac des Cygnes. Her legs two tallow candles, her diaphragm a wobble. At least that was how it felt.

"I was wrong," said Vladimir Stroganoff, standing in the wings, "I will apologize to Dumka. Doura is as good as Trefilova. Better," he said magnanimously as the white wings spread, the dark head lifted and the Swan Queen took her stage.

"Doura," breathed General Dumka, transported.

Out in the Gold Room fans forgot to wave and the weight of hereditary jewels lay unnoticed on brow, neck and bosom, and only the Tzaritza thought of the Tzarevitch and wondered when Rasputin would be down again.

On the stage the gathering of swans moved, arched and posed like the drilled swans of the Maryinsky. Never would you have guessed that their lake lay in Omsk. Moonlight persisted. The swans gave way to their Queen, shaking the diamond drops from her feathers—real diamonds. Behind her the watchful, richly encrusted shadow of the Prince. But to-night no one remarked that he was no Nijinsky. Not that he was for a moment.

And now the four cygnets, pattering and pecking, their pas-de-chats falling on the stage like lightly shod thistledown. Each dancer out doing her best, each out to rival Dourakova, straining for a perfection that could never be theirs, but getting nearer to it than they had ever done before. And four mamoushkas were happy women that night.

The fairy tale of tears moved to its tragic end. The curtain came down. The Tzar gave a deep sigh of satisfaction.

The Tzaritza sighed, too. What could be keeping the holy little father? The sewing wench?

The music came up and the curtain came down.

Sixteen curtains!

Grisha relaxed.

Seventeen . . . Eighteen . . . Nineteen.

"Dovolno," * said the Tzar to his generals.

Twenty.

"And they say my word is law," sighed His Imperial Majesty. He looked at General Dumka. "Ah, well." He joined in the clapping.

* * *

Divertissement.

Arenskaya was swinging a Spanish hip with verve if not precision.

"I say," said Bingo Haymarket, brought up against a background of "Pon my souls." "Now this is something like!"

* * *

Pancakes from the Tzaritza. Already they were sizzling.

But before this the presentation of the gold watches for the men and the diamond ciphers for the ballerinas.

First a blush of ballerinas for the ciphers. Then the line-up of the men.

"Nicholas Nevajno," called the Major Domo.†

* * *

* Enough.
† But it appeared that that one, having bumped into Rasputin, was under close arrest—Schmall scheque trouble.

And now the pancakes sizzling hot and bursting with cream, served by the Tzaritza sitting at the head of her table and carried along it right down to Little Igor by, with any luck, a Grand Duchess—at the worst it would be a Princess.

"At the Palace Sandringham," said Kashkavar Jones, "it is the porridge with the lumps that melt in the mouth."

And the Tzar strolled down the length of the table, talking to this one and that one, making the little jokes that his Court had heard so often. And he accepted a rose from Dourakova and sported it in his tunic, and he recognized Moysha Stroganoff, and he said, "Well, well, well!" and "How much did my little grandfather owe you?" And then he returned to the head of the table beside the Tzaritza, and he spoke to them all, and he thanked them for dancing for him, and he hoped that it would be possible for them to dance for him again, and he hoped that they would work hard and gain lustre for themselves and for Russia. And he sat down.

And General Dumka nudged the enthralled Vladimir's elbow three times, before the impresario realized he was expected to reply. And he struggled to his feet, and the long table dazzled before him, and brilliant impromptus tumbled over themselves in his mind, mixed with a reproachful incredulity at his failure to foresee this moment and prepare the words appropriate and buoyed up by the determination that his eloquence natural should still bear him creditably through.

Better make a start.

"Little Father of all the Russias," said Vladimir Stroganoff. "Little Mother . . ." He pulled his voice down. "May you live long in this land to bless us!"

To his own astonishment he found himself sitting down. His natural eloquence had indeed seen him creditably through.

★   ★   ★

Nearly time to go home.

The Tzar and the Tzaritza had retired and most of the Court had gone with them. The occasion was over, but the glory still abided. There is nothing so uplifting as glory without tension and the Company Stroganoff was excited and relaxed. And while the mamoushkas packed, the ballerinas flirted and the men swopped little stories, and old generals, who should have been in bed, were growing younger every minute.

But Natasha, though surrounded by generals, lacked her usual sparkle. She managed to smile and she teased them back and she parried invitations to little suppers all over the place, but underneath her near-radiance those five curtains were nagging at her.

She looked at Dourakova laughing up at Grisha. That one had made certain. She looked at her husband, perched on a piano and beaming at the whole room. Poor Vladimir . . .

In a corner Bingo Haymarket was taking out his monocle, gazing pinkly at Arenskaya, and putting it in again.

"I say," he said, "do you really want to go to England with me?"

"But all my life I have dreamed of it," said Arenskaya. "England! London! Piccadilly Square!" she envisaged, entranced.

Bingo blushed. You never knew with Russians.

"You'll come with me to England," he pressed. "With me," he underlined.

If Arenskaya got it, one couldn't see it.

"But, of course," she said. "Are you not a gentleman?"

From his cloud of bliss Bingo remembered. There must be no room for misapprehension anywhere. Only cads took advantage of innocence.

"You realize, my dear," he patted her pearly glove, "that when you come to London with me, I couldn't let you"— how to put it?—"meet the mater?"

"Qui?" asked Arenskaya curious.

* * *

Is it permitted to sing in Royal Carriages?

No matter. For on this occasion the ballet sang all the way home.

All save the little grandfather. He sat silent biting his nails.

"Little grandfather," said Vladimir, "what is the matter? Why do you not sing?"

"Son of my son," said Moysha sadly, "I am an old man. I could not remember how much the little grandfather of the Tzar, may his soul rest in peace, owed me."

"You do not remember?" said Aliosha incredulously.

Moysha shook his head. "I will not lie to you," he said. "I remember very well. But," he confessed, "my courage fail, and I say not one word to the Tzar."

"Steppe-land, my steppe-land," sang the carriages on either side.

"I am getting old," said Moysha. "I must go back to Omsk. On the business-man's train," he cheered himself up.

CHAPTER XXIII

A<small>ND</small> that, my friend," Stroganoff told the sandy man, "is how the Ballet Stroganoff danced for the Tzar. And there has been nothing in my triumphant career to equal that glory. And coming at the end of my first season in the capital, it crowned it with the jewel undimable and has set the standard of perfection that my company it maintain ever since." He thought of some of his performances. "Or tried to," he amended.

"You must have felt very proud," said the sandy man.

"And very happy," said Stroganoff. "And all that night my Natasha is very tender and very loving and she listen to everything that I plan for her future, and she do not call me a fool once." He sighed. "And yet, my friend, the next morning she is gone and there is only the letter she has left for me."

. . . I know you will think me cruel, Vladimir, but it is better so. . . .

A glorious morning. The sun streamed through the window when Stroganoff sat reading his letter.

. . . always you have done your best for me and always it has ended in nothing.

There was a knock at the office door. "Entrez," called Stroganoff automatically.

It was Dourakova. With her a very worried General Dumka.

"Vladimir," she said, "I must talk to you. They have asked me to return to the Maryinsky."

Stroganoff looked at his ballerina. "And what do you wish to do?"

"But to go back," said Dourakova. "What else could I wish? You understand, Vladimir . . ."

"Mais si," said Stroganoff. "I understand very well."

"I want to thank you, Vladimir," Dourakova extended her hand. "You have been a splendid colleague. You have helped me through a difficult moment." Tears came into her eyes.

"But what is this?" said Stroganoff. "You have helped me, too."

"Without you it would have taken me much longer to get back to the Maryinsky," said Dourakova.

"Without you," said Stroganoff, "I would be back in Omsk. Ah, well," he reflected, "there are, indeed, some worse places."

"Do not think me cruel, Vladimir," said Dourakova, "but I have to think of my career."

"Of course," said Stroganoff. "The career must come first." He nodded to himself. "The career before everything."

"I will always be grateful to you," said Dourakova.

"You can always return to me," said Stroganoff.

He rose. He kissed her hand. The interview was at an end.

But Dumka stayed on.

"You are not vexed, Vladimir?" he asked. "You do not hit the ceiling? My friend," he sat down, "you amaze me."

"What for I hit the ceiling when it fall on me?" demanded Stroganoff. "It is but natural this. When the bird it leave the nest it kick away the stepping stone. The stepping stone," he added, "it must look after itself."

"And it will," said Dumka defiantly. "Dourakova," he voiced a heresy, "is not the only ballerina in Russia."

"No," said Stroganoff.

"Courage," said Dumka. He wandered towards the door.

"Dumka," called Stroganoff. "I think we should make Dourakova the little souvenir. We owe her much. Go to Fabergé for me."

"Vladimir," said Dumka, "I love you."

He kissed him and went.

My husband:

When you read this I shall be on my way to Paris. I do not think you will be surprised except perhaps that I go so soon.

I have thought very long, Vladimir, but it is better so. Mamoushka is right. There is no future for me with you and there is no happiness for either of us.

I know you will think me cruel, Vladimir, but it is better so. Always you have done your best for me, and always it has ended in nothing. Always for you I will be the little wife first and the ballerina afterwards, and that way, Vladimir, it will not work. To Diaghilev I am a dancer and nothing else. If he did not think so he would not send for me.

This is the end of our marriage and do not think that I do not care—but my career must come first.

I do not think you will be unhappy too long. It is better so.

Natasha.

P.S.—It is better so.

Stroganoff held the paper closer. Yes, it was a tear mark.

A pair of arms twined themselves around his neck. Chypre de Coty! A large red mark planted itself on his bald dome.

"Vladimir," cooed Arenskaya. "You come with me to London?"

Stroganoff wrestled himself free. "Mais voyons," he said crossly, "is this the moment to make to me the project amorous?"

"Not you," said Arenskaya, "me I am faithful to my Bingo." She looked thoughtful. "Or will be."

"Bingo, Ringo—poof!" said Stroganoff. "My darling, run away and leave me to think in peace."

"But what is this?" said Arenskaya astounded. "Do you not wish to bring your company to London when I take so much," she coughed, "trouble to arrange it."

"Mais qu'est ce que tu me chantes?" said Stroganoff.

"London," said Arenskaya. "England. Bingo he has ask me to go with him."

"So you leave me, too," said Stroganoff. "Bon. Now I know."

"Au contraire," said Arenskaya. She stroked the evading bald dome. "I agree to go, but I tell him that he must take the company also."

The bald dome stopped evading.

"And he agree?" asked Stroganoff.

"He is very rich," said Arenskaya. "And," she eyelashed, "he can deny me nothing."

"And so, my friend," Stroganoff told the sandy man, "the Ballet Stroganoff came to London. Ah!—that Bingo Haymarket! He is the best backer I ever had. The money it flow like water till the family solicitor he put the foot down. Where," he gazed despairingly around, "shall I find such another?"

The sandy man changed the subject. "And Natasha?" he asked. "What happened to her?"

"What happens to any ballerina?" Stroganoff shrugged. "She dances for this one, and she dances for that one, and presently she has a daughter and then it is the daughter who must have the six curtains. When I meet her in Beirut after thirty-five years, it is the first thing that I hear. After that we remember the old days and we both cry a little." Stroganoff blew his nose. "Pure gold, my Natasha," he said. "I miss her very bad these thirty-five years—when I have time to remember."

Lord Streatham put a winning head into the room.

"Well?" he asked. "Settled your business? What about a drink on it?" he suggested sunnily.

"Business!" Stroganoff remembered something. "But that is what I am here to do. Where," he demanded accusingly, "is the rich one?"

Lord Streatham coughed. Stroganoff rounded on him. "What for I pay you the salary fabulous," he thumped the desk, "if it is not to bring the rich ones to this office when it is arranged?"

The sandy man shook himself into action.

"Well, Mr. Stroganoff," he said, "I've enjoyed our little chat very much. It has been," he searched for the word, "most instructive." He extended his hand.

Something hit Stroganoff. Maybe it was Lord Streatham's expression.

"It is you—the rich one?" he asked.

"Well . . ." said the sandy man.

"Ah," said Stroganoff, beaming vastly. "Why did you not tell me this earlier. Figurez-vous," he told Lord Streatham, "I have been telling him all our little secrets."

"Oh, my God!" said Lord Streatham. He sat down.

Stroganoff turned to the sandy man. "You understand, of course, my friend," he said, "that all that I tell you happen long ago when my fortunes sway in the balance and the little push in the wrong direction it is the calamity and me I am at the end of my beam. To lose a backer then was a misfortune. To lose one now—poof!—there are a dozen others."

"I'm glad of that," said the sandy man.

Lord Streatham looked elaborately at the ceiling.

"Yes, my friend," said Stroganoff. "To-day it is very different. My ballet it has the prestige, the renown, the tradition. Everything it run on greased wheels, and if, from time to time, we seek the little capital, what ballet company, I ask you, is any different?"

The door opened. A green baize apron came in. It consulted a slip.

"Seventy-seven pun' ten," it announced and started tugging at the desk.

Stroganoff laughed merrily. "I forget to send the cheque," he explained. He scribbled. "And here," he dug into his pockets, "is the little something for yourself." He inspected his coppers and slid them back. "Give him five shillings," he told Lord Streatham.

"Er," said Lord Streatham.

"Allow me," said the sandy man.

From that moment he was lost.

"My friend, I embrace you," said Stroganoff, rising from his desk as the door closed behind the baize apron. "We are now the partners. We are now the brothers blood." He did.

"Splendid, splendid," said Lord Streatham. "Let's have lunch on it."

"Wait a minute," said the sandy man. "I'm a business-man." He remembered something he had heard this morning on the subject. He blushed.

But Stroganoff had forgotten it long ago. "Even the business-man must eat," he said. "Come. You have the little lunch, with me," he underlined, "and after I take you to meet my company. The little Stroganova!" He kissed his fingers.

"Will she call me uncle?" asked the sandy man sourly.

"They will all call you uncle," promised Stroganoff. "We give for you the little party on the stage—you like that, no? Come," he linked arms.

"Wait a minute," said the sandy man. "Don't rush me. Don't rush me."

"Rush you?" said Stroganoff. "Me!" He looked reproachful.

"Rush you?" said Lord Streatham. "Him!" He looked shocked.

"Now see here," said the sandy man. "I don't say I will back your ballet and I don't say I won't, but I do say that I will decide nothing until I've seen the books."

"The figures," said Stroganoff indulgently. "But of course you shall see them. You shall see them any time you ask. But at the moment, my friend," he looked at his watch for the first time that morning, "it is quarter to three et moi, j'ai faim."

"Mwoh ohssee," said Lord Streatham.

"Oh, well," said the sandy man, slipping. "But," he said warningly, "I'll want to see the figures first thing after lunch."

"Bon," said Stroganoff. "After lunch."

He linked his arm. Lord Streatham linked the other arm. They led him out.

THE END